Harry Edge

FEIWEL AND FRIENDS
New York

A FEIWEL AND FRIENDS BOOK
An Imprint of Macmillan

SPRAY. Copyright © 2008 by Harry Edge. All rights reserved.
Printed in November 2010 in the United States of America by R. R. Donnelley
& Sons Company, Harrisonburg, Virginia. For information, address Feiwel and
Friends, 175 Fifth Avenue, New York, N.Y. 10010.

Library of Congress Cataloging-in-Publication Data

Edge, Harry.
Spray / Harry Edge. — 1st U.S. ed.
        p.   cm.
Summary: Disparate teenagers sign up for a three-week-long, city-wide
assassination game during a water shortage, with pressurized water guns the
weapons of choice, under the watchful eye of a mysterious game keeper.
ISBN: 978-0-312-61344-0
[1. Games—Fiction.   2. Interpersonal relations—Fiction.   3. City and town
life—Fiction.]   I. Title.
PZ7.E227Sp 2010   [Fic]—dc22   2010012574

Book design by Véronique Lefèvre Sweet

Originally published in the U.K. by Hodder Children's Books,
a division of Hachette Children's Books.

Feiwel and Friends logo designed by Filomena Tuosto

First U.S. Edition: 2010

10 9 8 7 6 5 4 3 2 1

www.feiwelandfriends.com

For Conor

WEEK ONE

MAC

Someone was after him already. The game didn't start until midnight tomorrow. There should be no immediate danger. Most likely, the assassin planned to follow Mac to his rented apartment, where he would lay in wait. But that wasn't where Mac was heading.

Mac stopped suddenly. No footsteps behind him. Was he mistaken? Mac got to the bus stop and put his hood up. It wasn't raining, but the air felt muggy enough for there to be a storm. The buses only ran for another hour. He wouldn't be able to get one back.

If the prospect was promising enough, Mac would find a hiding place. He didn't have to be back at work until two on Monday. By then, he meant to be at least two targets down.

The number 5 bus appeared at the far end of the street. Just then, the first drops of rain began to fall. First rain in weeks. It was warm, yet refreshing. As the bus came to a halt, a guy arrived from out of nowhere. Middle aged, bald, he paid his fare and sat three seats back from Mac. Was he the assassin? Mostly, it was young people who played the game, but there was no upper age limit. The rules only stated that you had to be over fifteen.

The light on the bus flickered on and off. A faulty bulb, nothing more. Raindrops glistened on the window, backlit by street lamps. When Mac got off the bus, the balding guy didn't follow. Outside, the rain had stopped almost as soon as it began. The evening had become even more humid, unseasonably sticky.

Mac examined his laminate. A scruffy guy with thick glasses had given it to him in the waiting room of a derelict bus station. For no good reason, Mac had been expecting a guy as his first target. Instead, the guy had given him a grown woman. Jal, aged twenty-four, worked in an elementary school and lived in a shared house on the east side of the city. Her name wasn't her real name, any more than Mac's was. Many Spray players chose three- or four-letter names or silly nicknames as their player ID. Jal was pretty, if the photo was anything to go by. Mac wondered what she did on Saturday nights.

He had checked the phone book. Her house was around the next corner. It felt a little evil, arriving at a stranger's house after midnight, staking her out. What if someone called the police? The authorities knew about the game. They had tried to ban it, but there was no law against people using water pistols. To stop himself from being arrested Mac only had to show his laminate. By giving their details, targets gave you permission to enter their house, as long as it was to spray, not steal. And as long as you didn't actually break in.

The house was a nondescript two story with red paint flaking off its brick walls. There was a light on inside. The curtains were half open. Mac ducked beneath the fence at the front and waited. After a while, he used his binoculars. That was her all right: Jal, with two guys and another girl. It looked like they were watching a movie.

Mac had confirmed his target. Now he needed a place to hide. He walked around the perimeter of the house until he found a back gate with no lock. He let himself in, hood up, hands thrust in pockets. The best thing to do would be to sneak inside the shared house, be ready to do her as soon as midnight struck tomorrow. But twenty-three hours would be a long wait, and he had just pulled a long shift. To play Spray, you had to be patient. The game was three weeks long and it hadn't started yet.

Mac would return tomorrow.

Saturday 11:52 P.M.
SHELL

"Where did you meet him?" Cliff asked Shell.

"A rundown garage near the mini-mart. He was wearing a Yankees cap and this disgusting old raincoat. Yours?"

"He had a false beard and glasses when we met, really obvious fake, like he didn't care who knew. About my height."

"Mine wasn't as tall as you. Maybe there's more than one."

"Who cares? Want to compare targets?"

Cliff gave her one of his easy, cheeky smiles. Shell and Cliff had rooms in the same dorm building but this was the longest conversation they'd ever had. Cliff usually gave the impression he was looking down his nose at her. His attitude made Shell come over all perky and girly, a side of herself she didn't like. Yet, recently, Cliff seemed to be interested in her. Earlier in the day, when they'd been testing out their water pistols at the city park, he'd followed her around until he'd given her a good soaking. Tonight, he kept flirting with her.

"I'll show you mine if you'll show me yours," he went on.

Shell was crap at saying no. But no, she decided.

"Maybe later," she said. Several boarders at the City Academy had paid their money and tried to register for the game. There was a limit of two hundred players. So far, only the two of them had been accepted. At some point, they might be up against each other. Secrecy, as Shell saw it, was essential.

Cliff put his arm around Shell. He was very touchy-feely with other girls but never, before, with her.

"Come on, Shell. You know you want to share."

Before Shell could reply, Maiko knocked on her door. Shy Maiko had also applied to join the game. She seemed an unlikely assassin, but Shell suspected she had ulterior motives.

"Hey, Maiko! Did you hear yet?"

Maiko tossed back her long, dark hair and shook her head.

"Look at this." Cliff handed Maiko his card. She read it out loud:

"Prak. Works in a bank, lives on the other side of town. That sounds like a high-rise building, Cliff. Could be a tough one."

"We've got twenty-four hours before the game begins. By Monday, I'll know his routine, get him on the way to work maybe."

"It's weird," Shell said, "knowing someone out there has my location and my e-mail and they're coming to get me."

"Not if somebody else gets them first," Maiko pointed out. There was a loud *ping* from her laptop. Maiko opened it. Cliff looked over her shoulder.

"Too late to back out now," he said. "That's your contact e-mail from the gamekeeper."

The Game Is On! read the subject line. Maiko opened it:

> Return-Path: <gamekeeper@assassins.org.uk>
> Received: from aamtain07-winn.ispmail.nodoby.com
> ([81.103.221.35])
> for <maiko17@hotmail.com>; 10:00:33 +0100
>
> Thank you for your contribution. You have been registered in the game that begins at midnight tomorrow. Please read the following carefully.
>
> You must be available to meet the gamekeeper at any time during the week before the game begins. He will e-mail you a time and a location where you must meet him the next day. At the meeting, he will give you a manila envelope containing a laminated card that displays the following:
>
> > Your first target's game name and a recent photograph
> > Your intended target's home address

Your intended target's work address

Your intended target's real name and contact details

Keep this card with you at all times. Your mission is to find and spray (by water gun, water balloon, or Super Soaker) the target.

You can hunt your target down however you see fit; you can pose as a delivery person and spray them when they open the door. You may disguise yourself and soak them in the street, etc. You may not hunt them down at work (or within a block of their work), at their place of study, or on public transportation (including waiting areas). Breaking and entering is also forbidden. Any infraction will result in disqualification and your target's reinstatement. You may work with other players, but there can be only one assassin, and only one winner.

Further refinements to these rules will be given to you with your target card. Rules may change or be added to. You must inform the gamekeeper of all successful soakings within four hours. Cooperation is mandatory. When you are assassinated you must surrender your target card to your assailant. If you are successful in your assassination attempt, the person you sprayed will give you their laminate. The person they were supposed to spray next becomes your new target. This continues until you have worked through all remaining players and retrieve the laminate with your name on it. At this point, you may claim your prize.

"It's so exciting," Maiko said. "Now all three of us are playing!"

"But only one of us can win," Cliff pointed out. "Let's make a deal. Whoever lasts the longest, the other two will help them. Deal?"

"Deal!" the other two agreed.

They began to discuss game strategy. It was just after midnight when Maiko's e-mail *ping*ed again. The new mail was from the gamekeeper.

> You are to meet me this evening on the third floor of the multistory parking garage at 216 City Road. I will be by the pay machine at 6:15 precisely. Do not be late or your place will be forfeited.

Her computer gave another loud *ping*. The three of them read the e-mail highlighted on the screen. The sender was anonymous. *You are my first target,* it said. *I shall take you out on Monday, at 12:01.*

Sunday 9:04 A.M.

GREEN

Two men stood outside the dorm building.

"Spray surveillance?" The dude talking had wiry hair and a thin mustache. Age: thirty at most. "Maybe we can help each other."

"Sure," Green said. He held out his laminate. This dude wasn't his target. "Let's see yours."

He looked at Mustache's laminate. Her Spray name was Maiko. She lived in the same mixed dorm as Green's target, on a girls' wing. She had no part-time job, unlike most students. Mustache wasn't allowed to break into her room or attack her in buildings where she studied, so she might be tricky to spray in the short term.

"I want to hit her at 12:01. Are you a student?"

Green shook his head. "I'm IT support all over the Academy campus."

"Nice. Means you can't be sprayed here. I have a plan."

Green listened. He had a few plans of his own. He was going to win this game. But you had to use other players. He was happy to steal their ideas. That was how you got on.

The plan was a good one.

"Okay," Mustache finished. "All we have to do is swap cards."

 Sunday 11:28 A.M.
HAN

"Are you the gamekeeper?" Han asked the clean-shaven man wearing thick, dark glasses.

"No. I'm his assistant. How old are you?"

"Nearly sixteen," Han lied. "Do you want a birth certificate?"

"No," the gamekeeper's assistant said. "I'm aware that you sent in proof of age and identity, but, in person, you look very young."

"I'm trying to," Han said. "That way, my targets won't notice me coming. I thought I might wear a school uniform some of the time."

"Most high schools have spring break soon," the assistant said. "A uniform would make you conspicuous."

"Thanks for the advice."

He handed her the card containing the name and details of her first target. Han glanced at the contents. It wasn't who she wanted.

"Thanks," she said to the man, whose shape and face were largely concealed by his coat and the woolen ski mask he wore.

"Good luck," the gamekeeper's assistant said. "I'm sorry to give you the information so late. We're short staffed. Please wait here for two minutes before leaving."

Han stood at the door, watching him go. He had sensed that she was too young but didn't seem to care. Not much, anyway. Behind her, in the musty, derelict church, a rat darted between the pews. Less than a minute had passed, but it was long enough. She hated waiting.

SHELL

Shell opened the door to a plump guy with dark, curly hair. She didn't recognize him. At first, she thought he was another student. She could usually tell students and civilians apart. The guy wore no-brand sneakers, a plain T-shirt, and baggy jeans. A screwdriver handle poked out of a front pocket. Not a student, Shell decided.

"I'm here to help with Maiko's computer," he said.

"Tech support on a Sunday?" This had to be part of the game.

"I was called in."

"Can you show me some ID?"

"Course."

He showed her a staff card that looked genuine, with a photo ID. As he was putting it away, Shell glimpsed another card beneath it, a credit card–sized laminate like the one the gamekeeper had given her.

"Can I take a closer look?"

She snatched the guy's wallet and, before he could object, had lifted the laminate high enough to read Maiko's name.

"Maiko's not in," she told him. "She's meeting the gamekeeper, getting her target details. So I'm afraid you're a little early." She turned around and yelled down the corridor. "Cliff!"

Cliff stumbled out of his room. "What is it?"

"You ought to meet this guy. He's Maiko's assassin."

"Really?" Cliff reached into his pocket. There was a whirring noise. The big guy seemed not to hear it, for he didn't hurry off. He had a sheepish smile on his face, like he'd been caught out but didn't mind. A real loser.

"It's only a game, right?" he said. "Spray and be sprayed. You playing, too?"

Cliff nodded. Before the fake tech guy could turn around, Cliff whipped out his phone and took a photo.

"Neat," the big guy said. "Let's see."

He leaned over and looked at the picture. "Not a bad likeness. See you later, dude."

"I hope they're all as stupid as him," Cliff told Shell when the big guy was gone. "One of us might have a chance of winning."

Sunday 10:39 p.m.
MAC

It was warm enough to be in shirt sleeves, but Mac wore an old gray windbreaker with big pockets. He had been home for sleep, a shower, a shave, and something to eat. The game started in eighty minutes. Jal—if she was here—would be on her guard. There were no lights on in the house. Mac guessed she was away, staking out her own target. Or she and her housemates might have gone out.

He tried the back door. Locked. He had two options. One was to sneak into the house when one or all of the residents returned from wherever they were. The other was to hide out. Jal didn't drive. He'd checked her route to work. A bus would drop her off within a block of her school, so he had to get her before she got on the bus.

He heard footsteps. One set. Was this her coming back? No. Too heavy. Mac crouched behind the garbage cans at the rear of the house. The back gate had been left open, not by him. He had a narrow view of the street. A silhouette passed. It could be, almost certainly was, the bald guy from the night before. Luckily, Baldy didn't pause, or look around, but kept walking.

Okay, so Baldy must live around here. No need to be paranoid. No, take that back; there was a need to be paranoid, but the guy hadn't spotted him. If he was playing the game, he was probably on his way to Mac's home, staking him out there. Mac had left a light on in his first-floor apartment. Let Baldy watch as long as he wanted. Mac had no intention of returning tonight.

The street was quiet again. Time to find a hiding place.

Sunday 11:58 P.M.
SHELL

"Why aren't you out stalking your targets?" Shell asked Cliff and Maiko.

"I've taken a look at mine," Cliff said. "There's no hurry. Everyone's going to be on their guard at first, running around like crazy. I plan to lull mine into a sense of false security."

"If your assassin doesn't get you first," Shell pointed out.

"We'll be fine if we stick together," Cliff said. "And we already know what Maiko's looks like."

"You could hardly miss him!" Shell said.

"He's there now!" Maiko said, pointing out of the window. "He said he'd get me at 12:01 and there he is, waiting to come in!"

Something felt wrong. *Nobody would be so brazen,* Shell thought, *no matter how stupid they were.*

"Let's go and scare him off!" Cliff said.

"I'll stay here with Maiko and watch," Shell told him. Cliff shot off down the corridor, yelling. Doors opened. Other students hurried out after Cliff, wanting to know what the fuss was all about.

"This is exciting, isn't it?" Maiko said. "I'm glad I let Cliff persuade me to join."

"You like Cliff, don't you?" Shell said.

"Everyone likes Cliff," Maiko said with a shrug. "Isn't he why you joined the game?"

"No!" Shell said as a crowd of students clattered onto the concourse outside the dorm. No campus security yet. The Academy authorities said the game was irresponsible. Bystanders could be frightened. But the Academy hadn't banned it.

Shell would run a mile from a real gun. But you'd have to be pretty dumb to mistake a brightly colored plastic water pistol for a deadly weapon. People might get wet; that was the only risk. And only if they got in the way of those who chose to play. The game was harmless fun, was how Shell saw it: a welcome release during exams. As long as assassins didn't spray each other in assembly halls and classrooms, there was nothing any authority could do to stop it.

She looked at her watch. Only a few seconds before the game began. Seven. Six. Five. Four. Three. Two. One.

Monday 12:00 A.M.
GREEN

Everything went according to plan.

Cliff, the arrogant guy who Green had met earlier, came charging down the stairs. There was a posse of students behind him, most of them giggling like infants in nursery school. They opened the security doors as wide as they went, then charged outside. None of them noticed the dude with the mustache as he weaved his way through the crowd, ambling into the building.

"Hi, man," Green said, affecting a laid-back, surfer drawl. Cliff gave him a smug grin. He was a year younger than Green, seventeenish, and, even if he was a straight-A student, no better qualified. But Cliff looked good and, in this world, good looks were all you needed to feel superior.

"You're not getting inside," Cliff told Green. "Maiko's protected. So you might as well go home. Leave her alone."

"I'll leave her alone, all right," Green said, pointing his Super Soaker. "She's not my target. You are."

As Green sprayed Cliff, the posse of students burst into laughter. Cliff, drenched, gave Green one terrible, furious look. Then he realized that he had to take his soaking lightly or he'd appear even more stupid.

"Oh, you conned me, all right," he muttered, shaking the water from his curly hair. "I suppose you want this."

He handed Green his target card. Green shoved the laminate in his pocket without a glance and walked away. The watching students applauded. All the hundreds of computers Green had fixed for kids their age and older, and nobody had ever applauded him before.

He wondered how the dude who'd helped him was getting along. What name did the mustachioed man go by? He should have asked.

Monday 12:01 A.M.
SHELL

Watching from an upstairs window, Shell wasn't sure whether to feel sorry for Cliff or pleased that he'd had his comeuppance. The boy who sprayed him was clever. He'd even showed them a laminate with Maiko's details on it. Which meant that he must be working with Maiko's assassin. . . .

Shell hurried up the stairs to the floor where she and Maiko had rooms. Maiko's door was ajar.

"Maiko. It's me, Shell. You've got to lock your door!"

"Too late," said a warm, deep voice.

The guy at the door had a pencil mustache and long, thin hair.

"He knocked on the door and I opened it," Maiko said. Her T-shirt was soaked through.

"I said I'd get you at twelve-oh-one," the shooter said. "Can I have your card, please?"

Maiko reached into her pocket. Shell only got the briefest glance at the picture on the card. A good-looking young guy. Mustache looked at her looking at it.

"You playing the game, too?" he asked.

Shell nodded.

"Catch you later," he said with a grin.

Monday 7:49 A.M.
MAC

Mac wished he had a car to sleep in. The shed he'd found was extremely uncomfortable. He'd spent the night scrunched up between a bunch of tools and an old bike. Now his legs ached. He was tired, but he was in position, crouched behind the garbage cans at the back of Jal's house. Any moment now.

A door slammed. Mac didn't know what the other people in the house did for a living, but elementary school teachers had to wake up early, so this was likely her. He lifted his head above the can's lid just high enough to see out. It was Jal, all right. She stopped at the front gate and looked cautiously up and down the street. She was within range. He had to move now.

Mac tried to stand. Disaster! His leg had gone to sleep. He leaned on the can, pressing his foot against the concrete, trying to get some feeling back. At least Jal hadn't seen him. She turned left out of the front gate. The bus stop was three hundred yards away. If she ran, Mac might not reach her. Still holding on to the can, he overbalanced. It fell onto him, bruising his thigh.

Nobody came out to investigate the noise. That was something. Mac forced himself to stand, then limped through the back gate into the street. He had worked out Plan B the night before. There were two streets that ran parallel to each other. If he ran fast enough along the back one, he could overtake her.

Mac had to work his way through the pain. He ran along the street, picking up speed, ignoring the puzzled glances of a postal worker on her rounds and a cyclist wearing a helmet. A tiny dog with big ears, perched at a window, barked loudly. As Mac passed, it scratched at the glass, as if about to leap through it. Mac turned the corner and almost ran straight into Jal, who was walking at a fast clip, her bus stop only a hundred feet away.

"Watch it!" she said in a stern, schoolteacher's voice.

"Sorry," he said. Pulling open his windbreaker, he revealed the pistol concealed beneath it. He gave it a couple of pumps, then sprayed her across the chest and shoulders.

Jal looked angry, angrier than he had seen a woman since his stepmom walked out on his dad. "How am I going to go to school looking like this?" she asked him.

"You should have thought of that when you entered the game."

"Touché." She shrugged hopelessly, her makeup running, then opened her purse. She got out the laminate containing the name of his next target. "Good luck."

Taking the laminate, Mac felt more alive than he had in months. He was aware of everything going on in the world around him. It was like being in the movies, in wide screen, high definition, surround sound, and even—sort of—cinematic slow motion. He was aware of Jal noticing something, reacting. What?

Mac spun around. The bald guy from the bus the night before was walking toward Mac. He had an orange Super Soaker in hand. In another moment, he would be in range. Mac tensed, scoped his surroundings. There was nowhere to run.

"Excuse me," Jal said, and stepped aside. "I don't want to get even wetter."

Mac was trapped. Baldy wasn't his target. Even if Mac's pistol weren't empty, he would not be allowed to shoot back. Mac had to take his punishment like a man. The only witnesses would be Jal and the cyclist wearing a helmet. The cyclist, oddly, seemed to be coming back in their direction. Baldy pointed his gun. Mac stood his ground. Braver to take a soaking than run and avoid the full force of the blast.

Mac managed to smile at his assailant. He felt like the condemned man facing the firing squad. But there was no shame in getting caught. At least he'd made one kill. The bald man's middle-aged face was serious, full of intent.

Before Baldy could press the trigger, the cyclist passed alongside him. The cyclist appeared to say something. Baldy turned to look at him, or her. The cyclist grinned and pressed a button on the bike's handlebars. A spray of water soaked the bald man. He dropped his Super Soaker, glanced at Mac, and shook his head.

The cyclist did a U-turn and returned to Baldy, who began to laugh in a creepy, empty way. Then he surrendered his card.

"Shouldn't you be running?" Jal said to Mac. "The cyclist'll be after you in a moment!"

Mac took another look at his new assassin but couldn't make out his or her face. Then he sprinted away.

Mac didn't look back, but ducked in and out of streets and alleyways, his heart pumping and head spinning, not slowing down until he was sure he couldn't have been followed.

Tuesday 8:50 A.M.
ZED

Their living space was a metal box, little more than six feet cubed, with bunk beds on one side and a fold-up table with laptop, radio, and electric kettle on the other. Their clothes were piled on the floor, except for their uniforms, which were on hangers at the end of the bunks. For washing, they had wet wipes. The portable toilet was for use only in emergencies. The overhead fluorescent light, leeching power from the street supply, flickered.

"When you suggested we move in together, this wasn't exactly what I had in mind," Zed said.

"In the future," Yogi replied, "most people will live like this, in storage containers. When you get a job in a different city, your home will be forklifted onto a flatbed and away you go."

"I think most people would want windows, if only for better ventilation. Still, it keeps us safe from our stalkers."

"How did it go last night?" Yogi asked. He'd been asleep when she got in. He slept like a log. Full of adrenaline, it had taken hours for Zed to pass out, hours listening to Yogi snore in the dark.

"I got him on the street. He'd been out on a kill himself, had a couple of drinks to celebrate success."

"Fatal," Yogi said. "Come on, details."

Zed gave him the details, downplaying what a thrill it had been, dwelling instead on the long hours she'd spent waiting behind a low hedge, doing occasional crunches to keep herself supple.

"How'd you do?" she asked when she'd finished.

"We're a team, right?" Yogi said to Zed.

"Until we end up facing each other," Zed said.

"So help me track down my target."

"She lives in a dorm at the City Academy, doesn't she? Can't be that hard."

"I went over there during work. There'd been reports of an

intruder and all the witnesses were really anxious to tell the story, make it clear that this was just a game. Seems there were three of them in the same dorm building playing the game. Two got blown away in the first five minutes. That just leaves my girl."

Zed laughed. "Five minutes! That was an expensive experience."

"My target's a science major. When I asked to see her, everyone closed up on me. I figure she might talk to a girl. . . ."

"More than half the people in the game are women," Zed pointed out. "They're protecting her, and they'll suspect me."

"Not if you don't have a Super Soaker on you," Yogi said. "Come on, you've made one kill already."

Zed smiled, remembering the sweetness of the feeling when she'd sprayed her target. She had the laminate for her next target, but he wasn't at home and didn't start work until this evening, when she, too, had to be at work.

"Okay," she said. "I'll see what I can do. Is it clear?"

Yogi raised the periscope. "Clear."

While Yogi dressed, Zed checked her makeup, zipped up her boots, pulled on her biker jacket, and unlocked the door of their immaculately concealed hideout.

"You follow thirty paces behind, like we agreed."

Yogi finished putting on his uniform. "You look nothing like your photo. You're being needlessly paranoid."

"Do you want my help or don't you? Peel off when you're sure I'm clear," Zed said. She pushed back her long hair to reveal the gold stars that studded each of her ears. "I'll see you tomorrow morning."

Zed stepped outside. A hot sun beat down on the city streets. When she was sure she was clear, Zed boarded a bus heading for the City Academy.

Tuesday 11:55 A.M.
SHELL

Shell was safe in the classroom and the corridor immediately outside. It counted as a place of study. Nevertheless, Cliff and Maiko walked her across the Academy campus. One strode in front, the other behind, ready to intercept any potential assassin. She'd thought of skipping the class but that was too paranoid. Her assassin would have to be very sharp to get access to her schedule. Also, walking around with a pair of bodyguards was a thrill. This feeling—like you were on stage all the time—was one of the reasons she'd joined the game.

"I'll meet you when class ends," Cliff said when they reached the lecture hall. A brief flash of resentment crossed Maiko's face.

The door was locked. It wouldn't mean anything that Shell didn't recognize the young woman who stood next to her. The Academy was very popular and new students transferred in all the time. The girl looked slightly older than Shell and was in

Goth gear. All black apart from gold studs and silver bangles, a leather jacket too heavy for the time of year, and round John Lennon glasses. Shell tried to spot where she might have a water pistol concealed.

"Are you famous or something?" the Goth asked as she pulled a small notebook out of her tiny bag. "Those two looked like bodyguards."

"Nothing like that," Shell said.

"Or maybe your boyfriend's just very clingy. He's a hunk, though. I wouldn't mind him clinging to me."

"He's not my boyfriend," Shell said.

Their teacher was nowhere to be seen. To avoid talking to the Goth, Shell reached into her bag for lip balm. Mistake.

"Is that a water pistol you've got in there?" the Goth asked.

Shell gave what she hoped was an aggressive look. "You don't belong in this class. So tell me straight. Are you my assassin?"

The Goth gave a wide-open smile. "I'm not. Pat me down if you like, but I'm not carrying. Here."

She held out a target card like the one Shell carried. Her target was a guy, not Shell.

"I'm playing the game, like you. Maybe we could team up."

"Where's your Super Soaker?"

Gothgirl shrugged. "My target's staying away from home and doesn't start work until this evening. No point in carrying it."

A man in a suit walked up to the door.

"I'm afraid Mr. Callan has been called away on short notice. Sorry for your wasted journey."

"My name's Zed, by the way," said Gothgirl. "Want to grab a coffee?"

Cliff was coming to pick Shell up at five to one. She had to hang around until then.

"Sure," she said.

Tuesday 12:10 P.M.
MAC

Mac's new target had an unfair advantage. Mac couldn't spray him at the office, or when he was sitting in the car, because—in his job—the car counted as a place of work. Not only that, but Mac didn't have a car himself. He couldn't follow the car until the target got out of it. People in the target's job shouldn't be allowed to play the game, Mac figured. He'd watched him go into the office; now he watched him come out. His cell phone rang as he unlocked the car. The target hunched his shoulders as he answered. Was this a chance?

It was a four-door car and a three-second run. Mac risked blowing his cover and ran. He opened the rear passenger-side door. The target wasn't too tall. The driver's seat was pushed a fair way forward. There was room for Mac to squash into the well between the front and back seats. He closed the door behind him and waited to see if he'd been heard. A car door opened. The passenger door.

"Get a move on!" The voice was loud. Mac had hoped for

time to get his Super Soaker primed. He wanted to make a kill as soon as the target got out of the car. But now he had to keep still and hope the Super Soaker's reservoir was sufficiently pressurized. There wasn't much space. Mac risked repeating the problem that had nearly cost him this morning's kill. Cramp. The other car door opened.

"What did the boss say about using your private cell on duty?" Loudmouth asked. He sounded a fair bit older than the target.

The target chuckled. "Not as much as she'd say if she knew what the call was about."

The engine started.

"You joined the game, didn't you?" Loudmouth asked.

"I'm planning on making my first kill today. A student."

"There's a special briefing notice in the patrol room. Watch out for idiots with water pistols. Members of the public might mistake them for terrorists or armed robbers."

"Sure. You get an awful lot of armed robbers using bright pink and green water pistols."

Pause, then Loudmouth again.

"Where are we going? This isn't our normal route."

"Just a brief detour. I got a tip."

As he drove, the target explained how the game worked, why he had to be part of it. Loudmouth wasn't impressed.

"Water pistols are wimpy things. Kids' stuff."

"They've come up since your day. Do you know how a Super Soaker works?"

"Science isn't my strong point."

"Air pressure. Each time you drive water from the large reservoir of your Super Soaker into the small reservoir, it pushes up against all of the air inside. Air is compressible—you can reduce its volume by squeezing it—but water isn't. The more water you squeeze into the reservoir, the higher the pressure of the air inside. This cushion of high-pressure air pushes on all of the water in the reservoir; the water presses on the sides of the gun, trying to get outside to restore the pressure balance."

"So why doesn't it leak?"

"The only thing keeping the water in the gun is the trigger," Mac's target explained. "The trigger works as a lever, pressing against the plastic tube that the water goes through. The stronger the lever, the better the gun. Release the lever and the pressurized air shoots the water out."

The car did a sudden swerve and Mac's Super Soaker rammed against his left kidney, making him groan. The guys in front didn't seem to notice. Mac's gun used CPS—the Constant Pressure System—his gun had a flexible bladder that kept the water under extra pressure. It was better at retaining water pressure over long periods of time. At least Mac hoped so. He hadn't had to field-test it yet. Also, the CPS had a bigger range and you didn't need to keep squeezing the trigger.

"I still don't get why you're playing," Loudmouth said from the driver's seat. "It isn't going to make you popular at work."

"The game makes you feel more alert, more alive, when you know that somebody's after you all the time," Mac's target said.

"Don't you get enough of that in this job anyway?"

"No, there's too much sitting around. Here we are."

"A café? Didn't you say places of work were out of bounds?"

"Classrooms and bedrooms are out, not coffee bars."

Mac heard a rustling noise. Something landed on the backseat. A tie. It was followed by a jacket. The target wanted to be out of uniform. The car door opened and closed. Mac had to risk getting up. He half stretched, half rolled onto the backseat. No way could he do this silently, so he spoke before he was spoken to.

"Don't panic," he told Loudmouth. "I'm part of the game."

The target's partner could grab Mac, warn Yogi in time for him to run. But Mac sensed that the two men weren't buddies. Mac gave the loudmouthed partner a big grin. The partner grinned right back.

"Go get him, cowboy."

Tuesday 12:21 P.M.

SHELL

Zed handed Shell a coffee and they sat in the window. They were too near the door for complete comfort. At least Shell knew there was a back way out. Zed had checked for her when she went to the bathroom earlier. If a threat appeared, they could bolt.

A police car pulled up outside. You didn't see them on campus very often.

"You should get yourself a CPS," Zed told Shell. "They've got a fifty-foot range."

That was exactly the kind of gun Shell had. Why did people always assume Shell was a wuss? She was about to explain this to Zed when she saw something that distracted her.

"Look," she said to her companion.

The policeman—if he was a policeman—was out of the car and walking toward the café. He wore an open-necked shirt and had his right hand behind his back.

"Oh no," Zed said as the policeman's right hand appeared, holding a bright yellow Super Soaker. She stood up.

A boy with scruffy blond hair was getting out of the backseat of the car.

"He's cute," Shell said. "Think one of them's after one of us?" She wanted to bolt but didn't want to miss the action.

"Doesn't matter," Zed said as the cute guy blasted the policeman with his Super Soaker. "Now *he's* got CPS."

Shell watched the soaked police officer reach into his pocket and hand over the laminate.

"His new target's bound to be you," Zed said. "Let's get out of here."

She opened the café door.

"What about the back exit?" Shell asked.

"This way's quicker," Zed said. "Don't worry, he hasn't had time to reload."

Funny, Shell thought, *the way Zed seemed sure that the target was me, not Zed herself.* Zed was a student, too, wasn't she? Shell got a good look at the blond guy as they hurried away. Behind him, another police officer, in full uniform, got out of the car. He was laughing his head off.

Wednesday 6:54 P.M.
HAN

"Where do you keep your weapons?"

"Would you like to see them?"

Han nodded enthusiastically. The assassin pulled out a large tray from beneath his single bed. It was covered with brightly colored plastic. He pointed at them one by one.

"This is a Super Soaker with a water burst attachment. This one's got a three-way directional head for shooting around corners. This is a standard water pistol for traveling. Only a fifteen-foot range but that's good enough for most assassinations. These are fake cigarettes with a built-in water pump. Over there's my supply of water balloons. And this is a standard Super Soaker."

"Can I hold it?"

"Sure."

Han lifted the empty gun. "How long does the contest last?"

"In theory," the hairdresser told Han, "the game could go on forever. Some people hide out and don't make any kills for the first few days, slowing everything down. That's why there's usually a rule that, if you have a week with no kills, you're out. Also, no two games are the same. In the final week, the gamekeeper always revises the rules a different way. First time, the person with most kills won. Next time, there was a last man standing, time-limited knockout. Ideally, it ends in a classic duel, a gunfight at the O.K. Corral kind of thing."

"You've read all this up, haven't you?"

"It's all on the Net. I can show you where to look."

"That'd be cool," Han said, flicking her hair back to let him see her wide-eyed smile. "What about the gamekeeper? Is he one person or a team?"

"As far as anyone knows, it's just one guy. He must have support. And money. The game takes place in cities all over the world. The entry fee isn't exactly high."

"Did you meet him?"

"He handed over my first target card. The way he was dressed, big coat, sunglasses, hat, I couldn't even be sure he was a 'he.' What about you? Did he give you my details in person?"

"No. By e-mail."

"Most stuff gets done by e-mail. I'm surprised he granted an interview to a school magazine, though. This game gets attention from all of the big papers and magazines. TV, too. It's a phenomenon."

"Really? How exciting," Han said. "Maybe he responded to me because I asked nicely. Could you do me a favor?"

"Anything," the hairdresser said.

"Could I try out the gun?"

Han was wearing her school uniform. She'd told her inter-viewee she was fourteen and that her dad was outside in the car (there was no car; no dad, either). As the hairdresser loaded the Super Soaker, she showed him a photograph.

"I don't suppose you recognize this person? They could be playing the game. It's a couple of years old."

Her target shook his head. He handed her the water pistol.

"Will you take a picture for the magazine?"

"Sure." He snapped her playfully pointing the Super Soaker at him.

She took the camera back. "Okay if I shoot you?"

"Sure. By the time it comes out, the game will be long over."

"I didn't mean with the camera." Han gave him a sweet smile before using his own water pistol to soak him.

Five minutes later, when the hairdresser had calmed down, toweled off, and given her his target laminate, Han made nice.

"I know you'll be following the game," she said. "If you come across the person from the photo, please e-mail or text me. Here."

She gave him the laminate with his details as a souvenir.

"How old are you?" he asked.

"Does it matter?" she said. "And do you think a real fourteen-year-old would turn up to interview you wearing a school uniform?"

She glanced at the laminate.

"Done any research on this guy yet?"

The hairdresser shrugged. "He lives in a very secure apartment complex, and when he's not there, he's working. Good luck. You'll need it. I can't see him falling for the interview scam."

"Don't worry," Han said, "I never play the same trick twice."

Thursday 12:11 A.M.
ZED

Finishing up a shift was the dangerous time. Zed knew she was being watched, but they weren't allowed to hit her in the building. Would her assassin spot her when she left? Not easily. She had called a taxi. Her plan was to swing by her next target's place on the way back, check it out. She had a pistol on her but wasn't planning to take her out tonight, not unless an opportunity presented itself.

Then she would go back to the hideout. Would Yogi be there? He had been eliminated, so there was no reason for him not to go back to his own place. She hoped he had. His joining the game was meant to bring them closer together, but he had screwed up from the start. She'd gift-wrapped Shell for Yogi and he'd bungled the hit by bringing his own assassin with him. You'd have thought, as a police officer, he'd be cleverer than that.

Zed changed into her street clothes, put her uniform in a

shoulder bag, and left by a maintenance exit. She spotted her assassin as she was getting into her taxi. He glanced in her direction then returned his gaze to the main entrance. Not a clue.

MAC

Work was a haven but hardly relaxing. Every time a bike passed, Mac went into a state of hyper alert, thinking this might be his assassin. The bike was his only clue. He wasn't even sure of the rider's sex. But s/he had sent him a text that morning, signed D.C.

You'll need cooling off after flipping those burgers, it read. *Soak you later.*

D.C.: Dangerous cyclist? S/he would be watching him now. D.C. would know that the burger bar closed at midnight on week nights, might follow him on the bus the way Baldy did. Mac was safe until he got on the bus. The stop was on the same block as the burger bar. But when he got off, he was a sitting target. So he had to find another way to get home, or set up a decoy. Also, he had his own target to track down. A seventeen-year-old student called Shell.

Shell had seen him. She was one of the two girls sitting in the window of the café at the Academy. She had hurried off with her friend, the Goth, as he was collecting the laminate

35

from Yogi, the game-playing police officer. He could have gone after her. Mac didn't have time to reload. Even so, he could have borrowed Yogi's water pistol and got two for the price of one. But it would have felt wrong, against the spirit of the game. Yesterday, he had been given a narrow escape. Today it was Shell's turn for the get-out-of-jail-free card.

Mac could wait outside her dorm all night, stalk her. But he wanted to play it smart. There must be a way of drawing her out. Mac had two hits already. If he could spray a policeman, he could surely soak a high school student. But, first, he had to avoid being soaked himself. He turned to Ben, his coworker.

"Can I stay at your place tonight?"

"You're hiding out because of your stupid water pistol game?"

"You'd find it exciting if you gave it half a chance."

"To each his own. It sounds like tag for grown-ups to me. But you can have some floor if you want."

"Where are you parked?" Mac asked.

"Back of the supermarket."

That was two streets away.

"Would it be all right if you left before me, picked me up from here?"

"What am I, your chauffeur?"

"I'm being hunted," Mac said.

"Okay, okay. You finish closing up tonight and I'll give you a lift back to my place. I've got a spare blanket."

"You're a pal."

Outside, a bike drifted by with no lights on. Dangerous.

GREEN

Green was famous for pulling late shifts. He liked his own company and, though things still went wrong at night, there was less to do. He played games, designed software, e-mailed and messaged buddies. Since finishing school at sixteen, most of his friends were people he'd never met. He was more comfortable that way.

This whole building was Green's work zone. When the game was on, work was the safest place for him to be. He had even started sleeping here. Green had a flashlight and a master key that let him into the bathroom. He had a sleeping bag and a pillow that he kept in the video recorder cupboard (nobody had used videos for years). He might stay tonight. Or not. It depended what he saw on the screen.

On Monday, while his target was at work, Green had erected two battery-powered video cameras outside his victim's riverside apartment. He'd leeched a wireless connection from her neighbors. For thirty hours, he'd had a high-res video feed of the front and back entrances. Not that there was much to see. He had only scoped her once so far. A car with shaded windows dropped her off after work on Monday. She was some kind of company director. The driver got out of the car, checked out the street, then opened the front door of the apartment for her. She rushed inside. Next morning, the driver collected her and they did the procedure in reverse. Yesterday evening, she didn't come home. She could be hiding out at a friend's, or she could be staking out her own target.

Academy security only did one circuit of the building after it closed, at ten. Green had hacked into their cameras, too. Thanks to them, he was pretty sure he'd discovered who his own assassin was. She'd been hanging around the main entrance yesterday. He'd also seen her peering into the IT suite earlier, trying to make him.

The assassin probably had him down as a big, slow-moving target. But Green had his moves. He looked at the bank of screens. No sign of his assassin. There was a light on in his target's apartment. Had he missed her going in, or was it on a timer? If it was a timer, he'd have seen it the night before. He rewound the recording until he saw a van in front of the main entrance. It had been there such a short time, he'd thought it was stopped in traffic.

A worthy opponent. He wondered how many kills she'd made.

Green wanted a night in. Some TV, a frozen pizza (no way would he risk having one delivered), and a couple of beers. If he was going to go home, it had to be now, before the building shut down. But Green didn't want to exit until he knew where his assassin was.

There! He caught her on one of the surveillance cameras, skulking near the front entrance. She dropped out of view almost immediately, but her body language had given her away, as had the baseball cap she always wore. Green used his cell phone to order a taxi. Then he rang campus security.

"Hi, sorry to bother you guys, but I want to report a suspicious person on campus. I'm pretty sure she isn't a student. . . ."

Thursday 10:32 P.M.

SHELL

Shell checked the game's Web site. The first kill reports were starting to appear. They were boastful accounts that used first names for both the targets and the assassins. Cliff and Maiko were among those listed.

Some of the assassins used pseudonyms online. One, calling him- or herself D.C., described stalking her target ("hard to miss, with his polished bald head") as he stalked his, and getting him just before he made his own kill, who was now her next target. Sometimes, targets shot back, making a kill into a water fight. But it didn't matter who shot first. If you got soaked by your assassin, you were out.

Shell had yet to sight her own target. She was wary of going out unescorted, so she'd shown Cliff her target card, and enlisted his help. She'd thought the game would make her brave. It was like the Web site said: Playing this game was like being in an action movie. Only Shell was the stereotypical female victim, the damsel in distress, the one the hero tried to protect. And Cliff, despite being out of the game, seemed determined to cast himself as her hero.

"Okay," he said. "I'm going to see your target. He went out for the evening, so he might be heading home pretty soon. Will you be ready to join me if an opportunity presents itself?"

"You bet," Shell said.

"I'll stay with you," Maiko said.

"Thanks," Shell said, though she didn't want Maiko around. Maiko was here because she wanted to get next to Cliff. And she could have him. Until today, Shell had felt indecisive about Cliff. He was convenient, but he didn't set her heart racing. As of this afternoon, she was much more interested in the guy she'd seen earlier. Another clichéd scene from an action movie: the girl who fell for her assassin. Although, in the movies, it usually happened the other way around.

"Give me a ring if he's waiting outside," she told Cliff. If the guy was there, she would go to one of the hall windows to sneak a peek.

"Sure," Cliff said, pulling the brim of his baseball cap down so that it covered his eyes.

"I wish I knew what my target looks like in the flesh," Shell told him. They hadn't spotted her once yet. All she knew was what was on the laminate. Name: Han. Age: 15. Occupation: high school student. Shell, Cliff, and Maiko had both hung around the exits to her school at the end of the day. None of them had spotted her. Han supposedly lived in an apartment, on her own. But she was never in.

"Maybe you should come with me to her place now," Cliff suggested. "Try to get her to come to the door."

"She'd never fall for it," Maiko said.

"And what if my assassin's waiting outside?" Shell asked.

"I'll tell you what," Maiko said. "Let's do an early morning attack. I have an idea how we can make it work. Up for that?"

"Sure," Cliff said. "But I'll go and check her out now anyway."

They agreed to meet at 6:30. When they were gone, Shell switched off her lights, then went to the window. A guy who had been standing under a tree abruptly turned and walked away. Was that her assassin? It was too dark to tell.

Friday 12:15 A.M.
MAC

Mac pulled down the shutter and waited for Ben's car. *It was lucky,* he thought, *that the burger bar closed at midnight.* Some places stayed open until one, even two. He'd chosen this job because it was the sort of place where they didn't check your references too closely. He'd lied about having experience. Luckily, you didn't need any experience to flip burgers.

No sign of the cyclist. It was another hot night, unusually so for the time of year, but very windy with it. Not a night for staking out a dormitory. *By now,* Mac thought, *D.C. would be*

41

outside his home. But s/he wouldn't have any idea where Ben lived.

According to the rules of the game, it was okay to spend one night away from your home. You must inform your assassin (via the gamekeeper) if you went outside the game area. In theory, if you were gone for two consecutive nights, you could be eliminated. However, this rule was unlikely to be enforced. After all, you could be on a stakeout.

The gamekeeper communicated solely by e-mail. Mac would check his at Ben's before going to sleep.

A car pulled up in front of him. Not Ben's. The door flew open.

"Quick!" said a guy in the backseat. "They're onto you. Get in!"

"What are you talking about?" Mac asked.

"Look behind you!"

Mac looked. Four people were running down the street. One appeared to be carrying a baseball bat.

"They want the keys. Come on. We're on your side. Get in!"

Mac's heart pounded. He was in danger, he knew, but where was the threat? The guys in the car or the guys on foot? Where was Ben? It was too late. The group with the baseball bat was almost upon him.

"It's your funeral," the guy in the backseat said, slamming the door. As the car drove off, the four guys reached Mac. They launched into a stream of obscenities that concluded:

"Give us the keys and get out of here!"

Mac stood his ground. He was pretty sure that he was being

set up. These guys were working with the guys in the car. And if this was part of the game, these four weren't allowed to use violence. But what if they weren't?

"This is your last warning!"

Should one of them hit him, Mac would run. Otherwise, he had to stay put. Where was Ben?

The guys surrounded him. They were all a little older and taller than Mac. Now he saw that the thing one of them—the leader, he assumed—held was not a baseball bat. It was a Super Soaker, extended length, special edition, blue and silver.

"I'd run away if I were you, squirt," the leader said, "or you'll get very wet."

"Do your worst," Mac said. "I'm outside my place of work. Soaking me here doesn't count."

At last, he heard the bronchitic engine of Ben's old car. Some instinct made him glance behind him. There, silhouetted in the car's headlights, was a cyclist. She or he waved. Mac waved back. By unspoken agreement, Mac's four pursuers began to laugh. The one holding the Super Soaker slapped Mac on the back.

"Worth a try, eh?"

SHELL

There was a gentle knock on Shell's door. Shell felt her heart thump. She wasn't expecting anyone. Maiko had gone to bed. What if the curly-haired guy had persuaded someone to buzz him in?

"Who is it?"

"Cliff."

She opened the door for him. "Any luck?"

He sat on the edge of her single bed. Shell took the chair.

"I hung around that seedy building for an hour. No lights. No noise. Either she's out stalking her own target, or she's laying low."

"Thanks for looking, anyway," Shell said. Cliff deserved a hug or something, but she didn't want to lead him on.

"We'll get her. Even if she's cheating by living somewhere else. Maybe it's time for you to get in touch with your target, taunt her. You have her e-mail and cell number?"

"I don't want to speak to her," Shell said, sorry to come off so wimpy. "I can't make myself sound threatening."

"Why don't we compose an e-mail together?" Cliff suggested.

"I dunno." Shell looked at her watch. Twenty past twelve. They were getting up at 6:30. But she wouldn't doze off easily tonight. She opened her laptop and sat on the bed next to Cliff.

"What should we say?" she asked as he leaned closer to her.

"How about *you can run, but you can't hide*."

HAN

GAMEKEEPER COMMUNIQUE NUMBER 1
Return-Path: <gamekeeper@assassins.org.uk>
Received: from aamtain07-winn.ispmail.nodoby.com
([81.103.981.35])
for <addresslist concealed>; 76:00:36 +0800

Four days in and already a third of you are gone. Most
of you receiving this are serious players with one, or
even two, kills under your belt. As for the rest—you
don't deserve to be in the game if you can't make a kill
by the end of tomorrow. If you don't make a kill by then,
your target will be reassigned, and you're out. Oh, and
those of you who gave fake details in order to join in,
you're out, too. What do you think this is, a virtual
game?

Han read the e-mail twice. All week, she'd been dreading the
notice throwing her out. But this wasn't it. The gamekeeper
was bluffing, she decided. He hadn't busted her or she would
have heard directly. Han didn't live where she had claimed.
There were bound to be other players in her situation. They
wanted to be in the game but didn't live in the city, so they got
a fake address. Most would stay with friends, but Han didn't
have any friends in the city, so she was squatting in an empty

apartment. She could have raised the money to rent, but that would have left traces, which she didn't want to do.

The squat had no electricity. That was okay. Han wasn't there much. She could recharge her laptop and phone when she went home. Spring break began today. Mom thought Han was off on a school trip until Tuesday. The cash fee Mom gave her for this had come in useful, providing Han with water pistols and other incidental expenses. If she survived into the game's final week, things would get a lot trickier. But Han's aim wasn't to win.

Han was leeching a wi-fi connection from an apartment across the street. Her only other e-mail was a threat, evidently from her assassin. *Threats were meaningless,* Han thought, then changed her mind. They were a way of raising the temperature. She e-mailed her target.

> Don't think that working sixteen-hour days will keep you safe. You'll be too tired to see me coming.

Then she shut down her laptop to save battery power.

Friday 7:30 A.M.
MAC

It was hot, even this early in the morning. Mac felt conspicuous in his oversized denim jacket, beneath which was concealed his Super Soaker. Ben had spent the night on his sofa. This morning, while Ben slept, Mac borrowed his car to get to his target's place, arriving just in time to see her head off with two of her friends. He didn't have a driver's license, but Ben didn't know that.

Mac followed them from a distance, like they did on TV, and nearly lost them a couple of times. Stupid thing was, the place they were heading for was two streets away from his apartment. He didn't see them park but saw the target's two friends on the street, talking to a postman. Money changed hands and the dude put on the top half of the post guy's uniform. Then he headed around the corner.

Shell was already laying in wait, hidden in a doorway, her water pistol in her hand. Mac tried to work out his tactics. He didn't know which building Shell's target lived in. He could drive up to Shell when she broke cover. But would it work? He'd have to find her, stop, roll down the window, and get out his pistol before spraying her. She'd have every chance to notice him and run away.

Mac should have persuaded Ben to get up and come with him. Might as well let Shell spray her victim, then catch her not

47

paying attention. That way he'd get the new target laminate from her. As far as Mac could tell, there was no advantage to be gained by spraying more targets than your competitors. Let Shell do the work and have her moment of glory.

Friday 7:51 A.M.

HAN

Someone knocked on the front door. Her first visitor. Ten to one it was her assassin, making good on the threat of the night before. Han looked through the door's fish-eye peephole. A guy, twentyish, in a postal worker's uniform. Should she ignore him? Han didn't want to give the impression that she was never home. But why would she get mail? Nobody outside the game knew that she lived here. And the guy looked very young for a mailman. She called out.

"I'm not dressed. What is it?"

"Letter that needs to be signed for."

"Put it under the door. I'll push it back."

"Sorry, I have to see you sign it."

"Tough luck. I'm in hiding. You've heard about this water pistol game that's going on all across the city?"

"I've heard about it, but I'm not in it, I swear." He held up his hands, which contained only a single letter. "Look, no water pistol. You're safe."

He'd reacted too quickly, Han decided, too smoothly.

48

"Sorry," she said. "I can't trust anyone, and I'm not expecting any mail. Why don't you push one of those I'm-sorry-you-were-out forms under the door and I'll collect the letter from the post office when I'm out of the game?"

"This is a guaranteed-next-day-delivery letter," the guy said, sounding a little too anxious. "It has to be in your hands today."

"Then whoever sent it shouldn't have insisted on it being signed for, should they?" Han argued, more convinced than ever that this guy was her assassin. "Look, I'm going back to bed. Forget it."

She went to the window. The mailman waited a while to see if she changed her mind. Then he went around the corner without leaving any kind of form for her to fill out. The mirror she'd positioned on the window frame showed him walking away. He didn't visit any other buildings. Han was about to go back to bed when she saw a girl with long hair step out of a doorway. She was carrying a Super Soaker. Now Han knew what her assassin looked like.

Friday 7:54 A.M.
MAC

Mac pulled up a few feet from the jacketless postman, who was waiting with the other girl, facing away from Mac. They were too preoccupied to turn around. *Any moment now,* Mac thought. He leaned down, grabbed his pistol, and pumped it a couple of times to ensure maximum pressure. He looked in the rearview mirror. Shell and her friend hadn't returned. They were probably celebrating while collecting the card off the victim. Mac shuffled from the driver's seat to the passenger seat, ready to get out. It would only take him a moment to exit the car, soaking Shell from head to toe.

A green car pulled up behind him. It was the car he'd been following, only now the guy who'd been driving was in the passenger seat. Shell was in the driver's seat. Damn! The guy got out, shaking his head. Shell stared straight ahead. Mac cursed. He hadn't expected her to be so clever. To get her in the car now would be too difficult. Shell would see him get out and lock the door before he got to her. Better to lay in wait for her on campus. Could Mac shuffle back into the driver's seat and get away without being noticed? He checked the rearview mirror. The postman put his gear back on while the guy got back into the car. Mac would duck, wait for them to get out of sight, then follow. With luck, he'd get her in the parking lot.

A horn sounded. Despite himself, Mac looked around. The green car was alongside him, rolling its window down. Shell gave him a big grin and a little wave. The guy—her boyfriend, presumably—pointed a Super Soaker out of the window. He sprayed the side of Ben's car. Shell pounded the horn again and sped off.

No point in following her. Mac drove around the corner. Had Shell just made a kill? If not, he might be in a position to check out the home of his next victim. These were old buildings, a couple of them derelict, all of them divided into apartments.

Any one of them could belong to Shell's target. Slowly, carefully, Mac drove back to his own place, circling around the block before parking outside, keeping a wary eye out for his own assassin, with or without her bike. But the only person he recognized this warm morning was the postman who had helped Shell earlier, going on his rounds.

GREEN

Green showered at work then, thinking he was safe, took the bus that ran from the Academy to the center of the city every fifteen minutes.

He knew as soon as he got on that he'd made a mistake. He was preoccupied with his target. She was hardly ever home and seemed to spend the time when she wasn't working stalking her own target. The video camera he'd trained on her apartment was a waste of time. She never took risks with her exits or entrances. The key must be to get her during work hours, but out of the office. Which meant he had to do her today or wait until Monday.

He'd taken a stupid risk. His assassin came from nowhere and got on the bus just before it left. She had jettisoned the baseball cap, but he still recognized her at once. She wasn't allowed to spray him on public transportation, but as soon as Green got off, he would be in trouble. Either Green had to stay on the bus until it reached the end of the line, or he would risk being sprayed.

He thought she'd take a seat by the door, for an easy exit. Instead, she came and sat next to him, then started talking like they were old buddies.

"That was a good move last night, getting security to kick me off campus."

She was about his age, snub nosed, kind of pretty. Small but built. Girls like this didn't normally talk to Green, not unless he was fixing their computer.

"So you aren't a student there?" Green said.

"No, I go to a public high school. Those rich kids live in a different world, don't they?"

"Tell me about it. Have you got any kills yet?" Green asked, keeping his voice low.

"You'll be my first. You?"

"One."

"Well done." She held out her hand. "I'm Jenny."

Her hand was surprisingly slender and cool. "Green."

"Nice name."

Green shrugged. "It's okay, I guess. My parents like it more than I do."

"What are they, ecologists?"

"No, fans of a British pop group from, like, twenty years ago."

"I've been watching you for four days," Jenny said. "And I like what I've seen. I'd like to get to know you when all this is over. Would it be okay if I called you?"

"You're just trying to soften me up for the kill." Green's words stumbled out.

"What if I am? I still like you."

Green felt himself blushing. "You can call me," he said.

"Thanks." There was a long, awkward pause before she spoke again. "How are you going to play this?"

"I haven't decided yet," Green said.

"This bus goes in an endless circle. Did you know that? We could stay on it all day."

"Then I guess we'll get to know each other pretty well."

Jenny grinned. She had a nice grin. "What kind of ticket did you buy?"

"Round trip."

She held out hers. An all-day pass. "Your ticket runs out as soon as we leave the central zone. I can get you thrown off the bus. Looks like I've got you trapped, big man!"

Friday 11:23 A.M.
ZED

"Let me help you," Yogi said as Zed raised the periscope of their storage container. The street looked clear.

"You're not in the game anymore," Zed pointed out. "You could lose your job. I don't want to be responsible for you getting fired."

"Let me worry about that."

"But I do worry. Anyway, it's cheating. You're allowed to have people help you, but a police officer? That's crossing a line."

"How about if I don't help you get your target, but I watch your back? If I'd had somebody watching my back I'd still be in the game."

"That makes sense, I guess. . . ." Zed didn't like to argue too strongly. Yogi was still her boyfriend. He'd stayed in the hideout with her last night but wouldn't tonight, because she was going back to the nurse's quarters, where she was supposed to live, in order to fulfill the game's residency rule. There was no point in playing a game if you didn't stick to the rules.

That said, all rules could do with a little bending.

"There is one other favor you could do me," Zed said. "You'll need to be in uniform."

"Anything," Yogi told her. "My shift doesn't start until one. Until then, I'm yours."

Friday 11:30 A.M.
GREEN

Jenny was so nice that Green was almost tempted to let her spray him. They talked about his job, movies, the shop where she worked, and where they bought their water pistols.

"Mind if I get up?" he asked when the bus reached the business district.

"Getting off?" Jenny asked, with a sassy twinkle in her voice.

"I'm going to change my ticket to an all-day pass."

"Good move. I'll be right behind you."

A trail of people were getting off the bus. Green stood but waited until those exiting were gone and the bus was loading before he went to the front. He had to push his wide body around the people who had just bought their tickets.

"'Scuse me. Coming through. 'Scuse me."

Jenny followed in his slipstream. This wasn't going to be easy. She had an open bag at her side. A Super Soaker or water balloon was bound to be within easy reach. A woman with a stroller got on and Green saw his chance.

"Let me help you with that," he said as she folded up the chair and sat her son down in an empty seat. Green took the folded chair from her. He lifted the contraption up.

"Thank you. That's very kind," said the young mother.

"Not really," Green said, looking behind him. The last person was getting on the bus. He only had a moment. Instead of putting the stroller down, he thrust it at Jenny.

"All yours," he said, and let go of it.

Despite herself, Jenny caught it. Green backed off the bus.

"Don't let her off," he called to the driver. "She's trying to steal that stroller!"

The driver gave Green a confused look. Then, as Green was hoping, he closed the door. Green strode into the busy street. By the time Jenny got the driver to open the door again, Green was out of sight. His heart leaped. Whether Jenny liked him or not, it was good to know he had a worthy opponent.

Friday 12:38 P.M.
ZED

Yogi met Zed on the corner by the hotel. He had questioned the hotel manager, as she'd asked, pretending her target was a witness he needed to find.

"His shift starts at one, so he should be here soon. Great timing."

Zed thanked him. "You should go. I can manage from here."

"If you say so. But first, there's someone I need to talk to. Don't look around yet."

Yogi charged off. Zed gave it a moment; then she turned to see what was going on. Yogi was in conversation with a slender guy who had a thin mustache and long hair. Despite the dry summer heat, he wore a trench coat. No wonder Yogi was suspicious.

How had Zed's assassin made her? He must be good. She had covered her tracks so carefully. Zed decided there was only one thing to do. She strolled off in the opposite direction, past the hotel entrance. She wanted it to look like she was running away.

When she was out of sight, she doubled back on herself. An alley ran along the rear side of the hotel to the service entrance. That was the way her target, a porter at the hotel, would come to work.

A hot breeze from a ventilation shaft ran down the alley, adding to the sultry heat. Zed rang Yogi on his cell.

"Did you get rid of him?"

"Sure. I watched him walk away. We could find an excuse to arrest him if you want. Concealed weapon."

"It's a game. The whole city knows about the game."

"Yeah, but everybody knows city cops are stupid. Love you."

"Love you, too," Zed said, though she had her doubts these days. "Can you keep an eye out until just before one?"

"That's why I'm here. We're around the corner from the station. I can be a few minutes late for my shift."

Zed already had a place to hide in, a big, metal Dumpster. The Dumpster was emptied daily so it shouldn't be too filthy. Zed opened the lid, took a quick glance at the disgusting debris clinging to the bottom, then clambered inside. Oh well. She was wearing old clothes. Being smelly was part of the price of playing the game.

Zed checked her watch. The more conscientious workers would be arriving for their shifts soon. She didn't close the Dumpster completely, but jammed the lid open with her pocket periscope. Then she pumped her Super Soaker, priming it for action.

Friday 12:51 P.M.

GREEN

The sleek black building soared so high, Green couldn't see its apex from the city street. His target worked on the twenty-third floor. He had never seen her in person, but should recognize her from a distance. Only trouble was, he had yet to observe her leaving the office at lunch. He might have to hang around until the end of the day. If he did that, there was a big risk Jenny would find and spray him.

One good thing about the target's office: It had no parking garage, only a covered drop-off bay at the front. So, wherever she parked, his target would have to leave the building by foot. Probably.

Green reexamined the target laminate. Age thirty, investment banker, single, narrow glasses. Whenever he'd seen her, she wore jeans, even for her high-flying job. She was cool, a big shot. In no other circumstances would Green get her phone number. He hoped his story was good enough to fool her.

Zed's cell vibrated against her thigh. She checked the message from Yogi. Her target was about to turn down the alley. She looked through the periscope. There were three men coming. All wore the porters' gray uniform. At this distance, Zed couldn't tell which of them was her target. She could spray them all but that was against the spirit of the game, and anyway, Yogi could be wrong. These could be decoys. She had to wait for them to get closer.

Her heart pounded against her chest. Any moment now. The periscope wasn't as effective as she'd hoped. The images were too small for her to make a definite identification. At a guess, her target was the man in the middle. He had his shoulders hunched and his head down, like he was trying not to be noticed. Yes, that had to be him. He was three paces away.

Zed withdrew the periscope and punched the metal lid open. The guys on either side of her objective looked shocked. As well they might. A tall woman with huge hair, a military jacket, and filthy jeans was pointing a giant red Super Soaker at them. She grinned. They broke to either side of her target. Zed squeezed the trigger.

The target ducked, then hit the ground. He tried to roll over.

But it was too late. He was already wet and getting wetter. The target put his hands up.

"Stop, stop! You win!!"

Zed hauled herself out of the metal Dumpster, bits of greasy paper sticking to her behind. She landed heavily on the ground, dusted herself off, and walked over to the very wet porter. His coworkers were grinning. Zed held out her hand. He shook it.

"Every day this week I got somebody to check that in there. Today, these two told me I was being paranoid. You were lucky."

"You make your own luck," Zed said. "Can I have your target laminate?"

"Of course."

The porter reached into his pocket for a wallet. From the other end of the alley came a call. Yogi.

"Hey, Zed. Gotta go to work. You be careful out there!"

"I will!" Zed called, taking the laminate.

She was about to read her new target information when there was a tap on her shoulder.

"We meet again," said the cool-looking guy with the mustache.

From his trench coat, the long-haired guy pulled out the biggest Super Soaker she'd ever seen. Its spray was so wide, so dense, that within a second she was soaked. She turned and tried to run away. This only made her backside even wetter than her front.

"Had enough?" asked the mustached man.

Zed nodded. She handed him the laminate, which he wiped dry. "You got me good."

"At least," the slim stranger said, "you have had the honor of being beaten by the game's eventual victor, the legendary Zorro."

GREEN

Green called his target's office and established that she was on her lunch break. Then he double-checked the location. The office building only had a single exit. At one o'clock, floods of people left through the double doors, but not her, not unless she was a master of disguise. If she were going out for her lunch, she'd have gone by now. It was time to activate Plan B.

The police station was a two-minute walk from the office. In the foyer, Green brushed past a very wet woman wearing a military jacket and filthy blue jeans. She was with an officer in uniform. The woman was either a Spray player or she had just taken a swim in the pool by the ornamental fountain. The uniformed officer was distracted. He seemed to be apologizing to her.

"I'll get you dried off."

"You said you could start your shift a few minutes late. I thought you were looking out for me!"

"I'm sorry, I'm sorry."

"I had two kills. It was going so well!"

"Will you get her out of here?" the desk sergeant called. "She's dripping all over the floor. It's a health hazard!"

"There's a bathroom through here," the officer told the woman, flustered. He turned to Green. "Can you hold this thing open?"

"Sure."

The officer swiped his card and the security gate opened.

Green had an idea. He was going to call his target on his cell phone, but this game was all about seizing your opportunities. He walked confidently through the barrier, following the wet woman. There were several open desks ahead to his right, but Green didn't want anybody to hear his call. This was lunchtime, so most offices should be empty. However, he didn't know the police's shift system. He'd never been in trouble with the law and didn't want to start now. The secret was to move fast, and with confidence. A door to his right was ajar. He prepared an excuse and pushed it open. Empty. Yes!

He closed the door and picked up the phone. Most places, you dialed 9 for an outside line. Here, it didn't work. He tried 0 instead. Success.

The phone was answered on the fifth ring. Green gave his target's full name and the name of the officer whose office he'd "borrowed," Inspector White.

"I'm afraid there's been a complaint about you."

"From who?" Her voice was clipped, calm.

"I'm not at liberty to say but it involves an allegation of assault."

"That's ridiculous. This must be some kind of a joke."

"I'm afraid not, ma'am. We have to take allegations of this sort very seriously even if we suspect that there may be ulterior motives."

"Ulterior motives? This is about the game, isn't it?"

"What game would that be?" Green tried to sound ignorant.

"How do I know that you're a police officer?"

"You can call me back on this extension if you want, ma'am,

but you must call me back at once. Otherwise I'm afraid I'll have to come and interview you in your office."

"This is nonsense. I'm calling the police station now."

She hung up. Green waited for the phone to ring. And waited. Was she going to call? Or was the police switchboard busy? He had heard stories of people making emergency calls and being kept on hold for hours. This was hardly an emergency but it was the police. Come on!

The office door opened.

"Who the hell are you?"

Green nearly panicked. He was used to working with teachers. If one of them found a stocky eighteen-year-old sitting at their computer, they assumed that he had a good reason for being there. But this guy sounded like a bully. Green gave the only answer he knew.

"Inspector White? I'm tech support. They told me there was a problem with this computer but it seems okay to me."

The inspector cursed. "Thing keeps freezing up. Annoying as anything."

"Is there a particular application you're using when this happens?" Green asked, knowing that, at any moment, the phone could ring and give him away. He had to get rid of this policeman pronto, or get out himself.

"Word processing's the only thing that's always on."

"You've probably got some kind of software conflict. There's a program I can run. Can you spare the computer for a few minutes?"

"How many are a few?"

"Fifteen, tops."

"Very well. I'll come back in fifteen. Thank you."

"No problem. It's what they pay me for," Green said.

The phone still didn't ring. Best to fix the computer if he could, so Green ran a quick diagnostic check. There was a common conflict. The officer was using the wrong version of a mapping program. Green downloaded the right one and replaced it. Two minutes' work. He picked up the phone to call his target again. Busy. What should he do now? Maybe it was time to get out of here.

The phone rang. Green answered at once.

"White."

The target apologized. "They kept me on hold. Look, I realize you're genuine but I guarantee that this is a joke."

"I see," Green said. "But we have to take all complaints seriously. Now, I presume that you don't want me to come to your office to question you?"

"That would be seriously embarrassing."

"Then perhaps you can get safely over here for a brief interview."

"I guess . . . I can call a taxi to our entrance. He or she's not allowed to attack me there. Can I count on you to cover me at the entrance to the police station? I'm sorry, I know it sounds silly. But this is a game that you have to take very seriously."

"Very well," Green said. "But please try to get here within ten minutes. I have a number of other people to see."

"I'm on my way."

"Call me on this number when you're about to arrive and I

can make sure there are no people with water pistols waiting at the door."

Was getting her to call him again ridiculously risky? Jenny would be impressed. Green sat at the desk and, to distract himself, goofed around on the Internet. He read the accounts of recent kills on the game's Web site. Some people were up to three already. One player was described as a "legend" who had won two previous tournaments. He called himself Zorro. According to the Web site, Zorro had long hair and a thin mustache. Green wondered if he was the guy who he had helped get into the Academy's dorm earlier in the week.

He was clearing the browser cache when two things happened. The phone rang and the door opened. Green answered the phone.

"My taxi's just pulling up. Do I ask for you in reception?"

"No need," Green said. "I'll meet you there." He cut off the call but kept talking. "Yes, I thought that must be the conflict. Before I reactivate the system I want to be sure that there are no more potential problems." He paused. "I see. Okay, thanks."

Now he needed to get out as quickly as possible. He stood up and spoke to Inspector White, who didn't look too happy about Green using his phone.

"All fixed. To avoid this sort of thing from happening in future, please check with us before you download any new software. I know it's inconvenient, but, in the long run, it will save you time and keep the department working within legal guidelines."

The officer gave Green a shifty look. Good guess. Ninety

percent of computer users, including police, had some kind of shady software. Now the guy couldn't wait to get rid of Green.

"That's most helpful, thank you. Now if you don't mind, I . . ."

"I'm already late myself," Green said. "I'm out of here."

He hurried back out of the office, hoping he would be able to intercept his target with the water pistol concealed in his baggy jeans.

ZED

Zed left the women's restroom at the central police station. She had dried herself off the best she could, leaving her with ratty hair and a particularly smelly left leg where she had brushed the inside of the Dumpster. Yogi was waiting by the main entrance, looking anxious. He was supposed to be out on patrol, not looking after his humiliated girlfriend.

"You got two kills," he reassured her. "That's two more than I did."

"Thanks for reminding me I'm going out with a loser!"

A woman charged through the door. She looked like a lawyer—fancy, with expensive glasses. And she sported a telltale bulge in her large Gucci bag. Seeing Zed clocking her water pistol, the woman's gaze moved to the fluorescent handle poking out of Zed's shoulder bag. The woman began to back into the door.

"It's cool," Zed called. "I just got eliminated from the game."

The chic woman forced a smile. She turned to the desk sergeant. "The officer said he'd meet me out front."

The sergeant gave a pretty good approximation of a growl.

"Which officer would that be? Presumably one who knows you're trying to enter a police station while carrying a concealed weapon."

"Um..." The woman wasn't going to snitch on the officer by giving away his name. The desk sergeant started to go off on a rant.

"Because I am pretty fed up with constant security alerts caused by a childish game that involves people pretending to be terrorists while wasting gallons and gallons of tap water, of which, in case you hadn't noticed, there is a shortage. And this officer here is already thirty minutes late for his shift because he's been helping his very wet girlfriend get dry which she could just as easily have done at home. But if you'd care to tell me which officer has promised to protect you, I'll buzz him—and I presume it is a him because my officers only tend to make a fool of themselves over women offenders—and get him to come and collect you. But only if he can make it through me, first!"

The desk sergeant paused for breath and, as he did, noticed someone behind Zed. "You, did you want something?"

Zed, Yogi, and the water-game woman turned to see a fat guy with long hair and the world's baggiest jeans. He had a zen smile and his hands in his back pockets. His voice was high, a little nervous.

"Sorry to interrupt, but is this lady here to see Inspector White?"

"I am, and I have less than half an hour of my lunch break left. Where is the inspector?"

"He's waiting on the other side of that door, ma'am. I don't know how you missed him."

"Oh."

"If you'd just go ahead of me."

"Very well, but I thought we were meeting in–"

The fat man interrupted her. "You can't take that water pistol inside a police station, ma'am, it counts as a concealed weapon. That is a water pistol in your handbag, isn't it?"

"Yes, but . . ."

"Just go through that door, please."

Yogi and the desk sergeant exchanged bemused glances. As he followed the woman through the door, the fat guy began to pull a long, thin Super Soaker from the back pocket of his jeans.

A moment later, they all heard an angry scream.

"Why couldn't you be more like him?" Zed asked Yogi.

Saturday 9:14 P.M.
SHELL

The e-mail from the gamekeeper was very clear. Either Shell got a kill by midnight tonight, or she was out of the game. The gamekeeper, unlike her assassin, had her cell number. She could get a call eliminating her at any moment. And her target wasn't home. Shell hadn't even set eyes on her yet. The only proof of

Han's existence was that Cliff had spoken to her through a door.

Han, whoever she was, didn't have a job, and didn't appear to attend the school she claimed to attend on the target details. But she lived where she was supposed to live–Cliff had spoken to her, in his postman disguise. So Shell couldn't report her for cheating. Shell had one chance. She'd managed to talk herself in to a house across the road from Han. From here, she was within range to soak her target at a moment's notice. If she came home. And if Shell's own assassin didn't get her first.

Saturday 10:43 P.M.
MAC

"You want fries with that?" Mac recognized the guy he was serving but he wasn't sure where from.

"Yeah. So you haven't got her yet?"

"I beg your pardon?" Mac took the guy's money.

"My girl Shell. You're stalking her, right? I'm Cliff."

Mac remembered him now. "Are you in the game?"

"Got taken out."

"Bad luck," Mac said, though this guy looked like the lucky type–more likely he was out because of bad play. "How did you find me?"

"Spotted the car down the road. Total giveaway."

Mac hadn't thought of that when he borrowed Ben's car.

Stupid of him. What was this guy leading up to? Mac made conversation.

"Thought I had Shell the other day. You guys were too fast for me."

"Might as well give up now," Cliff said. "Her protection is too good."

"Hard to protect someone all the time," Mac pointed out. "How many hits does she have?"

"None of your business," Cliff said, taking his change. He hesitated. "You seem like a smart guy. What are you doing working in a place like this?"

"Lots of smart people work in places like this," Mac pointed out.

Cliff gave a brief nod, then left. Mac was good at reading people. Cliff's visit had told him two things. First, Shell wasn't Cliff's girlfriend, not yet, anyway. And second, Shell hadn't made her first hit yet. So chances were she was still stalking the place he'd nearly caught her at yesterday morning. Question was, could he get over there without alerting his own assassin, the anonymous cyclist? He turned to Ben.

"Can you give me a ride tonight when we finish our shift?"

HAN

In a dark, expensive city bar, the guy with the shaved head and the heavy gold jewelry was showing off to anyone who'd listen.

"My assassin will be waiting for me outside my house. But I've got no intention of going home tonight. I've got two kills already. This is my night off. Only question is, who will I be spending it with?"

The woman he was flirting with gave a fake smile, then turned back to her friend. Certain she'd found her target, Han took the free seat to his right. It was a risk. This was a twenty-one-and-over place. Even in this low light, and with the amount of makeup she had on, Han couldn't pass for eighteen, never mind twenty-one, not close-up. Whereas her target was almost thirty. She didn't know how to talk to a guy like this. She didn't know how to talk to a guy at all. She got out the photo she always carried with her.

"Excuse me. While you've been playing this water pistol game, have you come across this guy?"

Han's target glanced at the picture; then he glanced at her, to make sure that she wasn't carrying. He took in her tight dress and tiny purse, decided that he was safe. "He's a player?"

"I think so. He's an old friend I need to track down."

"Need? Sounds urgent. Tell you what, give me your number, I'll call you if I see him."

"That's nice of you, thanks. But I can never remember my number. Give me yours and I'll call you."

He did, and she typed it into her phone.

"Maybe I can buy you a drink," he said.

"A lager would be great." Han didn't want the bartender looking at her and she needed to get to a tap, so she made an excuse.

"I just need to visit the little girls' room. Back in a sec."

In the restroom, the water pressure was really low. It took Han a couple of minutes to fill the balloon she had hidden in her purse. When she'd got it to the bursting point, she tucked the bloated balloon behind her back and returned to the bar. Her target was paying for the drinks. He had his back to her, with his phone out, ready to take her number. Han stopped at the far end of the long bar. She couldn't resist using her free hand to text him: *Got you at last.*

"You were going to call me," he reminded her as she sat down and took a sip of her drink. His phone vibrated. He smiled again, then checked the message. Han smashed the water balloon all over his shiny head and trendy suit. Her victim swore.

"What the hell do you think you're doing?" the bartender asked. "I'll call the police."

"Be my guest," Han said. "And while you're at it you can tell them what you were doing selling booze to a fifteen-year-old girl."

It annoyed her, having to add a year to her age, but she didn't want her target to know she was too young to be in the game. Humiliated, the soaked slaphead handed over his laminate without protest.

Han hurried out of the bar before the situation turned nasty. She could have pumped her victim for info about her next target but she wouldn't trust anything he told her. Time to return to her stuffy squat. She would e-mail the gamekeeper with news of her triumph.

Saturday 11:59 P.M.
SHELL

The building's occupants were away for the weekend but had lent Shell a key. She could get into the stairwell, but not the apartment itself. There was a peephole through which she could see her target's place and whoever came to the door. She'd been looking through it for two hours and needed to pee.

Just before midnight, there was a light knock on the door. Shell let her visitor in.

"You're safe," Cliff assured Shell. "Mac's shift doesn't finish until one tonight, so he can't get away for another hour. And he's paranoid about his own assassin."

"It's nice of you to come," Shell said. "I thought you were going out with Maiko."

"A bunch of us went to the movies, but I made an early escape. I put you first," Cliff said.

Shell didn't know how to interpret that. She knew how much Maiko liked Cliff but not how much Cliff liked Maiko. Or her. If Shell didn't encourage him soon, it might be too late. But she couldn't make up her mind. And maybe that meant he was wrong for her.

"There's a way you can help me," Shell said.

"Anything."

"I think she'll come back in a taxi and only stop if the road is clear. Then she'll use the taxi for cover while she slips into the building before I can get across the road to spray her."

"So what do you want me to do?" Cliff asked.

"Delay her. Wait in the street where you can't be seen, then block her door when she gets back."

"She'll assume I'm her assassin."

"Exactly. While she gets out of your way, she won't be looking for me."

Sunday 12:21 A.M.
MAC

"No cyclists in sight," Ben said.

His car was in front of the burger bar with the engine running.

"Let's go."

"Hey, what's going on?" A male voice.

Mac twisted around, worried that the speaker was his assassin. But he recognized this guy, a regular.

"You're supposed to be open until one on Fridays and Saturdays!"

"I know, I know, but these are special circumstances."

"Can't I just . . . ?"

"Sorry." Mac pulled down the metal shutter. "You can buy a microwavable burger at the gas station down the road."

"I don't have a microwave."

"They'll heat it up for you there."

"I don't want to walk to the gas station. Do you know how hot it is out here?"

"So get an ice cream instead," Mac said, padlocking the shutter. "Gotta go."

As they drove off, Mac passed a posse of people on the corner. One of the silhouettes looked familiar. It was D.C. He still couldn't work out his assassin's gender. Mac was trapped by his shifts. D.C. was bound to catch him sooner or later. How was anybody supposed to win this game? That was it, Mac decided. He was always going to quit the burger bar when the game was over. But his game would be over much quicker if he didn't quit now.

Sunday 12:31 A.M.
HAN

Han didn't go straight back to the squat. The club where she'd sprayed her victim was on the far side of town. Han used her bus pass to check out her next target. He wasn't home, which was probably for the best. Han had only one spare balloon on her and balloons were only good for close work. She would collect her Super Soaker and return the next day.

Han caught the last bus and got off two stops from her place, where there was a taxi stand. The bus conductor had given her a funny look when she flashed her child's bus pass—not many kids under fifteen were around after midnight. The taxi driver gave her an even funnier look when she told her how short a distance she wanted to travel.

"You can walk there in five minutes."

"I know, but I don't feel safe. There are people after me. I want you to park right in front of the building and wait until I'm safely inside. Can you do that for me?"

The woman gave her a sympathetic look. "I'll do it, no charge, but take a bit of advice from me. You're never going to be safe in an area like this. How old are you? No more than fifteen, I'd say. Haven't you got some family you can go back to?"

"I do. I'm going home soon," Han said.

But not, she hoped, too soon.

76

Cliff waited outside Han's place. He tensed up when he heard a car coming. Not many car owners on this street. Could be her.

Tonight could be the night Cliff made out with Shell, but only if she had a successful hit. Cliff couldn't tell how much Shell liked him. It turned him on that she was in the game when he wasn't. And neither was Maiko. Maiko was beautiful but she kept making it clear that she had a crush on Cliff. For some reason, this was an enormous turnoff. Whereas Shell never flirted with him, rarely even smiled, no matter how much he helped her out.

A taxi rounded the corner. Han, the target, sat in the front passenger seat. This was going to be easy, if they played it right. As the car stopped, a phone rang. Nearby, but not his. Cliff didn't dare step out of the doorway to find out where the noise was coming from. At least Han couldn't hear it, not while she was in the taxi.

The phone stopped after the third ring. The taxi door opened. Han got out. Seeing her for the first time, Cliff was impressed: black cocktail dress—very elegant, not your typical assassin. Han slouched like a sulky teenager, rather than the smart ninja assassin Cliff had built up in his mind. She couldn't know she was being watched.

The taxi door stayed open. Han didn't appear to have paid yet. But she was almost at the door of her building. Timing was everything. Cliff made his move. He charged out of his shaded doorway, almost smashing into Han.

"Who the . . . ?" Had Shell been standing in the shadows, she would have sprayed Han by now. Where was she?

"What is this?" The taxi driver was getting out, a phone in her hand. "I'm calling the police, I warn you."

"No need!" both Cliff and Han said at the same time. Han, close-up, was surprisingly young. She reminded Cliff of his little sister, who was fourteen. But you had to be fifteen to play this game. The girl looked Cliff up and down.

"Where is it? Your water pistol?"

"I'm not in the game," Cliff said. He pointed over her shoulder. "But she is!"

Shell was holding her Super Soaker but did not point it. The taxi driver, seeing Shell with the gun, seemed to get the message.

"You're all playing that stupid water pistol game. I should have known. Biggest water shortage in the country's history and a bunch of kids decide it's a great time to waste water by spraying each other on the streets!"

She got back into her car and drove off, the passenger door bouncing shut as she rounded the corner at the end of the street. Han was fumbling with her key to get into the building.

"Spray her!" Cliff shouted. "Spray her!"

Shell shook her head, and the girl was gone, inside the house.

"I set her up for you!" Cliff said. "What are you doing?"

Before Shell could answer, another car turned the corner.

"Quick!" Cliff told Shell. "Get back inside! That guy's your assassin!"

"He can have me," Shell said.

"What's got into you?" Cliff asked her. "Why have you given up?"

The car pulled up alongside Shell. Mac, the guy from the burger bar, stepped out of it. Shell put her hands up. Mac looked surprised, like he couldn't believe his luck, but he pressed the trigger. He had his pistol set to intense stream. A thick torrent of warm water belted Shell. Mac seemed determined to empty his chamber. His spray moved up and down Shell's body, giving her a full soaking, from head to toe. Shell smiled like she was having fun.

"That feels great," she said. "It's been so hot all day."

Mac smiled. "You're taking it very well. Can I have your laminate please?"

"I'm afraid not," Shell said.

The smile faded from the assassin's face.

Shell explained. "The gamekeeper called me five minutes ago. Since I haven't made any kills in my first six days, I'm eliminated from the game. So your soaking me doesn't count."

The guy driving Mac's car called out to him. "Did I hear right? This was a wasted trip? We risked closing early for nothing?"

"Afraid so," Mac told him.

"I've had enough of this. I'm going home. You coming?"

"I just need to talk to this girl for a minute."

"I'm going now. If you want a lift home, get in!"

"I can't go home," Mac said. "Too risky."

"Suit yourself." The guy in the car drove off.

Mac shook his head. "So who's my target now?" he asked Shell.

"Dunno, sorry. I guess you'll get an e-mail about it tomorrow."

"Let's hope I can find somewhere safe to read it. Anyway, you had me going there. So you're not exactly a loser."

"And you could still win."

"Yeah, only I don't have a target or a safe place to hide."

"Do you want somewhere to hide tonight?" Shell asked him. "It's the weekend, so there are lots of empty rooms in our dorm."

"Really? That'd be great. Where is it?"

"Cliff will give you a lift. Won't you, Cliff?"

"Eh, yeah, sure," Cliff said, though he didn't like the way this guy seemed to have taken a shine to Shell. The wet girl, together with her new friend, got into the back of Cliff's car. So much for tonight being his lucky night.

Sunday 11:34 A.M.
GREEN

The doorbell rang as Green was getting out of the shower. Nobody visited him on a Sunday. Most of his friends slept even later than he did. Suspecting a trap, Green nearly didn't answer it, but the second ring was more insistent. He pressed the intercom button.

"Who is it?"

"It's Jenny, from the bus the other day."

"That's nice," Green called back. "You'll understand why I can't let you in."

"I'm safe," Jenny said. "I've been assassinated."

Green hesitated. "How do I know you're not bluffing?"

"Have a look at the game Web site. I was sprayed last night."

"Thanks," Green said. "But let me take a look at the site first."

He pulled on some jeans and a sweatshirt while his laptop booted up. No time to dry himself properly. Was this girl interested in him? What could she see in a fat slob who repaired computers for a living? More likely this was a trap. But no, there it was on the site, a boastful account of how this dude who called himself Drizzabone had "offed" Jenny by hiding in her parents' garden and catching her on her way back from a failed attempt at her target.

Green opened the door to Jenny. She was wearing exactly the same clothes combination as him.

"Either you're really good at hacking Web pages or you were eliminated from the game on Friday," Green told her.

"I thought I ought to warn you what your assassin looks like."

"Nice of you, but he's already had thirty-eight hours to spray me." Green felt bad about moaning. He really liked this girl.

"Not really, since you worked a double shift yesterday."

"How do you know that?"

"I persuaded one of the tech assistants in audio-visual that you were my boyfriend."

"What?"

"I did this little girl act like I was worried that you were cheating on me because you worked all these odd hours. So she told me I could check your schedule with her any time and what a nice guy you were and she was sure you wouldn't mess around."

"Clever," Green replied.

Jenny got out her phone. "Here's your new assassin."

She transferred two photos to his laptop.

"Anyone you've seen around?" Jenny asked.

Green shook his head. The guy had studs in his eyebrows and a barcode tattooed on the side of his neck. That was so last century.

"Maybe you could use a little help," Jenny suggested. "And it so happens that I suddenly have time on my hands."

WEEK TWO

HAN

Han was pretty sure she'd had a narrow escape. Who was the guy who jumped out from the doorway and why had his girl-friend not sprayed her? It made no sense, but it was a lesson. She would be more careful next time she returned to the squat.

Han had to stay in the game if she was to find Chris. She'd shown her fourth target the photo yesterday, directly after spray-ing him, but he didn't recognize him. All he'd said was: are you sure you're old enough to be in this game? But he didn't com-plain. Who wanted to embarrass themselves by revealing they'd been taken out by a fourteen-year-old girl?

Han checked the game's Web site. More than half the play-ers had now been eliminated. She was one of only three people on four kills: The others were Drizzabone and The Invisible Man. The leader, with five kills, was someone who called him-self Zorro.

Time to go out and track her fifth target. According to the game's Web site, she had only made one kill, on the game's very first day. She called herself Dangerous Cyclist. D.C. for short. Han had questioned yesterday's target—a dentist who she'd tracked down on the golf course—about her. The target said he'd only glimpsed D.C. twice. She wore androgynous clothes and a helmet that hid her face. She had a team of helpers, who stuck with her much of the time.

"You've got no chance," the target told her. "You might as well give up now. I did."

Second Monday 8:23 A.M.
MAC

"Wakey wakey."

Mac rubbed his eyes and pushed down the duvet cover. Shell had let herself into the room. For a moment, he couldn't remember where he was. This was the second dorm room he'd stayed in. Each had an identical layout.

"Thought I'd better get you up," Shell said. "You're meeting the gamekeeper to get your new laminate soon, remember?"

"Of course."

"Have you thought about where you're going to go after that?"

"Not really."

"After you went to bed last night, I had a word with a few other people in the corridor. They're cool with you staying as long as you don't let any of the staff see you."

"That's great. It's so much safer and . . . nicer here than my place. Only, I have to show my face there every other day, or I'm breaking the rules."

"When were you last there?"

"Thursday."

"Looks like you've broken the rules already, but this cyclist who's after you hasn't reported you, has he?"

"No. I guess not."

"You know what they say. Rules are made to be broken. Want some breakfast?"

"That'd be great."

Twenty minutes later, Cliff was giving him a lift to a café a couple of miles from the Academy.

"Shell seems to like you," he told Mac.

"It's all right," Mac told him. "I'm not trying to steal your girlfriend."

"Thanks," Cliff said. "I appreciate that, but she's not really my girlfriend. We're just friends."

"I'll put in a good word for you when I can, if that helps."

"I don't think she's interested that way. But anything we can do to help you, I'm cool with it. Now that we've been eliminated, you're our only connection to the game."

"Thanks," Mac said, faking enthusiasm. He'd managed to team up with three players who didn't have a single kill between them. "The main thing you can do is keep an eye out for suspicious cyclists."

GAMEKEEPER

The gamekeeper had a whiteboard where he kept a list of assassins and their targets. Now that more than half the players had been eliminated, he updated it constantly, shuffling names around until he could see the state of play. The first time he ran the game, he'd tried to keep it in alphabetical order, but that meant rewriting everything, several times a day, and it was still easy to make mistakes. Now he added the changed targets wherever there was a gap. Soon, there would be more gaps than there were players left.

> Han–Dangerous Cyclist
> Badmonkey–Famefan
> Dangerous Cyclist–Mac
> The Invisible Man–Obelisk
> Deniro–The Cartoonist
> Green–Deniro
> Senile–Suburbgirl
> Zorro–Factoid
> Mac–The Invisible Man

The gamekeeper wrote the name Lol, then checked his watch for the second time since arriving. He and his assistant had four new laminates to give out today. It was easier to make new laminates than it was to collect the old ones from players he had eliminated. The losers tended to resent being thrown out. Some of their complaints were valid. The gamekeeper did keep some of the game's rules vague, and he hadn't publicized the *no kills in six days and you're out* rule before play started. Each game was different. He had to ensure that the game worked its way to a thrilling conclusion within the three-week time slot. That meant adapting to circumstances.

This time around, a lot of players were being cagey, more concerned about not being sprayed than they were about spraying their targets. Maybe it had something to do with the heat wave, the water shortage. But such things happened every year in most countries where the game was played.

This game meant more to the gamekeeper than other games because it was in the city of his birth. He had been away a long time, and it had changed a great deal, but it was still home. One day, he would give up the game and settle down somewhere, maybe go back to school or start a business. This could be the place. And one day he would like the world to know he'd been part of this game, long before the rip-offs that were bound to come: the dumbed-down movie version, the reality TV series, the things the media did to make the wonderful commonplace, the weird the same, the whole world over.

"You're late," he snapped at the youth who joined him in the bus terminal.

"Sorry, rush-hour traffic."

"I have other people to see. Here's your new laminate."

"Thanks." The guy, who called himself Mac, stared at the gamekeeper. They hadn't met before. The gamekeeper's assistant had handed out most of the laminates, but had had to return to his own country for work. Now the gamekeeper was on his own, which got a little boring and lonely at times.

"You're younger than I thought," Mac said.

The two men were the same height and could almost be brothers. The gamekeeper should have disguised himself more. Today, he'd put on glasses with the plain lenses but hadn't bothered with the hat or the raincoat. They would have made him too conspicuous in this heat, so he'd gone for a green hoodie and jeans.

"Everyone tries to look older than they are," the gamekeeper replied. "Until they start trying to look younger than they are. In my experience, very few people are happy in their own skins. Are you?"

"I don't know what happiness means," Mac replied. He glanced at the laminate. "This Invisible Man, how many kills has he got?"

"I can't give out information that helps a particular player," the gamekeeper told him. "You'd better check the Web site. But be wary: Not everything people claim on there is true."

"Thanks for the warning." Mac leaned forward and shook the gamekeeper's hand. Surprisingly few people did this. They thought the gamekeeper wasn't a human, like them. He was a bit part actor in the role of an avatar. Sometimes the gamekeeper felt that way himself. Mac's handshake, like the gamekeeper's, was firm.

"Good luck," the gamekeeper said in parting, surprising himself, for he never had favorites.

GREEN

Green sat in his office, waiting for Jenny to call. He was good at waiting. Here, he was safe from Drizzabone. He'd always been cautious. Had to be. Big men made easy targets. He'd always been big, heavy. Heavy people were more likely to fall through thin ice.

Green didn't like being a wimp. By playing this game he hoped to turn one of his weaknesses—his hesitation—into a strength. And it was a thrill. He'd never felt better than he did after spraying the banker at the police station. Telling Jenny about it, watching her eyes light up as he described how he set her up, that was a thrill, too.

Green had never had a girlfriend, never really considered romance a possibility. So far, he and Jenny were just friends. But when he saw that glow in her eyes, anything seemed possible.

This afternoon, Jenny was out helping him to track his next victim. Green was using the Academy's surveillance cameras, on the lookout for Drizzabone. It was handy Jenny had taken that photo of his assassin, since there was nothing about him on the Web. The game's site held only the stark information that he was in joint second place. Green, with only two hits to his name, would be way down in the rankings. But it was where you finished that counted.

Green's next target was the trickiest yet. Deniro drove a taxi for a living, so her place of work was mobile, as well as invulnerable. He didn't know how many kills she had, but he knew she must be good to make it through to the second week. He would have to be better.

It was a pity Green didn't drive; that would make things easier. He'd had lessons, but most cars were a really tight squeeze for him. He'd tried cycling and quite enjoyed it, but people stared and smirked when he wobbled past. So he'd taken to less public forms of transportation.

He was still trying to work up a plan when his phone rang.

"She's got a husband who works at home," Jenny told Green. "She stopped by for lunch but he brought it out to the car, sat there, and ate it with her. They were looking around all the time. It's not going to be easy to get her. She'll need to get out to use a bathroom sometime, but we've no way to follow her 24/7."

"Never mind," Green said. "I just had an idea. How are your acting skills?"

Second Monday 6:11 P.M.
HAN

D.C. was tall, with a strong jaw and high cheekbones. She lived on a block overlooking the river. The water didn't offer much of a view. Over the last few weeks it had become a mucky trickle. The discarded junk of generations of city dwellers poked up from the riverbed. There were still crayfish and other hardy creatures for the anglers to catch, but only the suicidal would risk eating them.

The key, Han decided, was to find out where D.C. kept her bike. D.C.'s apartment was on the eighth floor, so she was unlikely to keep it there. And if she did, she would have to carry it down by elevator, making her vulnerable. The bike made her hard to hunt down on the road, but before she was on the road it became a weakness. Han had to find it.

The buildings were newish, expensive. D.C. claimed to work as a bike messenger but you needed serious money to live here. Either D.C. had rich parents or she was messengering goods that were both illegal and very expensive.

Han walked along the riverbank. This gave her a good view of the rear of the block where D.C. lived, but no access to it. Han had to walk onto a footbridge, climb up, and then go back along a road. As she did, a cyclist hurtled past her on the bike path. Was that D.C.? Han had no way of knowing.

Should Han spray this cyclist at random? It made a kind of sense but could get her into trouble. The bike helmet concealed the cyclist's head. A loose body suit in red fabric made it hard to tell if Han had just been passed by a man, or a flat-chested woman. Even so, Han had an instinct that this was her target.

The apartment block, like many built this century, had a series of big, secure lockers for residents to keep their bikes in. The lockers had no labels, only numbers and swipe-card readers. You couldn't see inside them. Han decided that she needed somewhere to hide. But first, she was going to take a look at D.C.'s place.

In the apartment building's airy courtyard, Han stood by the elevator. She got out her phone and pretended to make a call, waiting until a resident came by. He used his swipe card to summon the elevator. Han followed him in when it arrived.

"Eight, please."

On the eighth floor she walked down a long, airless corridor until she found D.C.'s number, 845. She knocked on the door, just to be sure nobody was there. Han could have rung the buzzer downstairs, but she didn't want to give herself away if D.C. was in. Whereas now, if Han pretended to be a neighbor, there was a chance that her target would come to the door. A tiny chance. You weren't allowed to break in and spray someone, but if a target was foolish enough to open their door, spraying them was fine.

No reply. There was nothing to stop Han from breaking in and snooping around to get intel on her target. Except the law, of course, but Han had a fake ID and wasn't bothered by the law. She was only bothered about whether she could use her credit card and pocketknife to finagle the lock on D.C.'s door.

She couldn't. The lock was strong and sophisticated. The door fitted too closely. Han's only chance of spraying D.C. inside this building was to chat up one of the neighbors, see if she could hide in an apartment as her last assassin had tried to do. But that approach hadn't worked when the girl student tried it on Han and it was unlikely to work on D.C. Moreover, even if she got in, Han would be stuck inside, with no sure way of telling when her target was coming. Besides, what she really wanted to do was to locate Chris.

You didn't need a swipe card to go down the elevator or get out of the building, so Han made a hasty retreat.

In the elevator, Han thought about her real target. There was a chance that Chris had not registered for the game. But she doubted it. Han remembered how, when they first read about the Spray game, Chris became obsessed. He would haunt Web sites, play endless videos, join fan forums. Han was sure Chris would have registered. Only death would stop him. And if he was dead, she would have heard. Chris might have been knocked out of the game already, but Han doubted it. Chris was smart enough to get to the final rounds. And so was she.

Second Monday 7:45 P.M.
GREEN

The heat had yet to drain from the day. Green waited in the shadows of a recessed doorway. The store it opened into had closed a few minutes before. The street beyond was nearly deserted. Green had an escape plan ready if Drizzabone came looking for him, but he didn't want to use it.

Green worked in this store a couple of days a month, on his days off, giving computer advice to wealthy shoppers. The manager had offered him full-time work, which paid better than the Academy, but Green wasn't interested.

If Drizzabone sprayed Green here, it wouldn't count as a kill. Technically, this was Green's place of work. He had listed it on his game application. But that felt like bending the rules. He'd rather not put the situation to the test. He had, therefore, taken extra care not to be followed when he got on the bus.

Deniro's taxi pulled up just before eight, as Green and Jenny had planned. He could imagine the dialogue inside the car.

"Wait here a minute, please," Jenny said. "I want to be sure the store is still open. They keep changing the evenings they stay open late."

Jenny got out of the car. She was slender and tough looking, the sort of girl Green fantasized about: He couldn't believe she was with him. She may only be here because she wanted to stay close to the game. She wanted to pick a winner: so what? Green was going to win. By the time he did, maybe Jenny would like him for who he was.

Jenny got out of the car and seemed to stumble. The taxi's windows were shaded. Green couldn't see the driver's reaction, but she must have seen it; she must be concerned. After a moment, Deniro rolled down the window. Good. But Green wasn't allowed to spray her in her car, because it was a place of work.

"Are you okay?" the taxi driver called.

"No. I hurt my . . ." Jenny put a hand to her head.

"Get back in the car. The store's closed. I'll drive you to a doctor."

"Thanks. I . . ." Jenny took the hand away from her head, having burst the fake blood balloon she'd pressed against it. As the dark red stuff gushed down her face, Jenny fell. She hit the ground so hard that Green was momentarily concerned for her.

Oh, she was a good actress, all right. It was going to be great having her on his team.

Deniro, looking anxious, hurried out of the car over to Jenny.

"I'm going to call an ambulance. Speak to me. How the hell did you manage to do this?"

Jenny blinked one eye open. "I didn't," she said. "Sorry."

Green let loose with his Super Soaker. He unleashed a strong spray from his primed Power Burst Pistol, deluging the taxi driver. The overspill washed the fake blood from Jenny's face.

"Enough! Enough already!" Deniro told them. "You got me. I was on the lookout for that woman in the fancy suit. She kept trying to flag me down and find an excuse to get me out of the car. So you must have already sprayed her?"

"Certainly did," Green said.

Deniro nodded appreciatively. "How many kills are you on?"

"You're my third. You?"

"Four. Wait a minute."

She got back into the car and came out with a cleverly designed water pistol the length of a car seat, with a long, narrow shaft and a fat, stubby hand piece that acted as a reservoir.

"It only holds a quarter of a gallon, but it has great range. You're going to need every advantage you have if you're going to get this guy." She handed Green her laminate. "He's a tough one."

Green read the laminate, half hoping it would be the guy he'd met on his first kill, the guy who he'd since worked out called himself Zorro. But this guy was much older, older than Green's parents.

"The Cartoonist," Green said. "He reminds me of that guy from the TV. What's his name?"

"Can't remember," Jenny said, "but I know who you mean."

"People often give really bad photos on purpose," Deniro told them. "I've never seen this guy up close. He lives in a high-security building."

"He has to go out sometime," Jenny said.

"Only at night and only, as far as I can tell, when he's on an assassination job. Look at the game Web site. He's on four kills, too."

"I'll get him," Green said confidently. "Thanks for being a sport."

"Don't thank me. Thank your girlfriend. She's a good con artist."

Green grinned at his target. "Any chance of a ride home?"

"As long as you've got the money to pay."

Green had enough. He had a return bus ticket, but he figured the taxi fare would be worth it for the extra information he'd pick up about the Cartoonist. Anyway, he couldn't take Jenny on public transportation with her clothes still smeared by fake blood. People might think he'd done it to her.

GAMEKEEPER

They were falling like flies. Since the gamekeeper eliminated all players without a hit, the remaining players had been busy. He had accepted 200 entrants. Three quarters of them had already been sprayed. At this rate, the game might finish early. On the Web site, defeated players had opened a book on who would win. Zorro was the favorite, closely followed by the Invisible Man. But the Web site was full of misinformation. The third favorite was a player who claimed to have four hits, but—as only the gamekeeper knew—didn't actually exist. Or if he existed, was using a different name.

He had seen it in other cities. There was a flurry of publicity and people tried to crash the game. Suddenly there were people with Super Soakers in plain view. It only added to the excitement. Without their laminates, the wannabes couldn't participate, not even if they got lucky and sprayed an actual player. But they added to the general confusion, which only made the game more interesting.

He turned on the TV. The main story was the nationwide drought. Reservoirs were at their lowest levels since records began. The government was talking about bringing in water rationing. Supplies would be cut off for large parts of the day.

"The hose and car-washing ban is no longer enough," the head of the department of environmental protection said. "I am asking people not to take baths and to limit their showers to a maximum of four minutes. But if we don't get rain by the weekend, we will have to take more drastic measures."

The chirpy newscaster came back on. "Before the weather report, there are some people who don't seem bothered by the water shortage—players of the world-famous water-war game that came to the city last week. Police say that numerous incidents involving water pistols have been reported, but there have been no injuries." She grinned at the cameras. "That is, unless you count injured feelings. Take a look at this footage, shot in the doorway of the city's central police station yesterday at lunchtime."

The gamekeeper smiled as a well-dressed woman was soaked by a fat guy in overalls. Who was that big man? He checked the wall chart, which had photo IDs by each name. The guy called himself Green. Three kills. His next target was hard, but all targets were hard at this stage. The gamekeeper took a look at who his assassin was. A nobody. Maybe Green had a chance. Anyone with the chutzpah to do a hit in a police station had to be taken seriously.

"He really is invisible," Shell told Mac. "Either that or he doesn't exist."

"According to his profile, he's thirty and he lectures at the City Academy. How can he be invisible?"

"Half the staff there seem to be somewhere else half the time. When I went to his office, there was a sign up saying that he's away all semester on 'research leave.'"

"But if he's playing the game, he must be around. Cliff and Maiko are both willing to help stake out his home address."

"But what if he's not there?" Mac asked, adding, "I'm never at home."

"Cliff said he'd drive you around there later if you want to check your mail, get some stuff."

"Good old Cliff."

Shell frowned. "What's that supposed to mean?"

"Only that he seems awfully anxious to help."

"I suppose he's still trying to make up for being knocked out in the first minute of the game."

Mac laughed. "I think his motivation might be more straightforward than that. He wants to keeps tabs on what you do with me."

Shell didn't know what to say to that. It was true, she had a crush on Mac. But Mac only treated her like a friend. Give it time and he might notice how her eyes lit up when he came into a room. Maybe he'd noticed already but wasn't interested.

There was a tap on Shell's door and Cliff pushed it open.

"I got something!" he announced. "Look what I found!"

"Where did you get that?" Shell asked.

"I went to the sociology department where the Invisible Man works. This was on the bulletin board." He handed Mac the notice. "That's his real name, right?"

"Oh yes," Mac said.

"Sounds like an interesting seminar," Shell said. "Pity it's three days away."

"And remember, we can't get him at work," Mac said.

"Yes, but you can get him on the way to or from work," Cliff pointed out. "At least now we know that he's around."

"So you're good for the surveillance tomorrow?" Mac asked.

"I'll do the first shift, at sunrise. Maiko will relieve me at seven thirty, then Shell at nine."

"Great."

"Can I have the flier?" Shell asked.

Cliff handed it to her. She pinned the poster to her wall. The title of the seminar was:

Water Wars. How water pistol games have sublimated the violent urges of a generation and become THE game of the twenty-first century.

"It's good of you to come this early," Green told Jenny.

"No worries. I know you have to be at work at one. This morning could be our best chance for a while. Did you bring it?"

"Oh yeah."

Green got out the laptop and showed her what to do.

"Make it as obvious as you can. If we can draw him out . . ."

"He'll definitely think that I'm in the game and will spray him."

"You're right," Green said.

"Unless I dress like this." Not sparing Green's blushes, Jenny pulled off her sweatshirt and tracksuit bottoms. Beneath them, she wore a skimpy orange bikini.

"No way I could conceal a Super Soaker in this, right?"

"Eh, right . . ." Green said, hoping that his face hadn't turned as red as it felt to him.

Jenny grinned and put her clothes back on. "By the time we get there, it'll be so hot outside that half the city will be wearing swimsuits. Maybe we can hit the pool after we've sprayed him. Have you got some trunks?"

"Eh, somewhere."

"Dig 'em out, big boy. We've got time."

While Green got out his swimming trunks and a towel, Jenny

went to check the street outside. She came back to tell him that it was clear and their taxi was waiting. Her smile was so wide, Green felt like he could conquer the world. But the pair of them still had to find a way into the Cartoonist's building.

SHELL

The young couple waited outside the Invisible Man's house.

"Maiko said she'd be here," Shell told Mac.

"We're late."

"I'll call Cliff on my cell," Shell offered. She did. It went straight to voice mail. She tried Maiko instead. It rang several times, then cut off. Call refused. Shell figured that she and Cliff must have finally gotten together. Well, good for them.

"I think it's just you and me," she said to him.

"There's no need for you to stick around," he told her. "If you want to get back and join your friends at home, I'll understand."

"I'll help you out until you get eliminated," Shell said. "That's if you want me to . . . quick, kiss me!"

"What?"

Shell flung herself at him, letting her long hair cover his face. She wrapped her body around his so that, to anyone passing by, the main impression would be of a very pretty, affectionate girl sucking the face off a hapless boy. After thirty seconds, Shell took her lips away and looked over Mac's shoulder once more.

"It's all right, she's gone."

"D.C.?"

"Thin, wearing red, helmet, green racing bike."

"Sounds like D.C."

"I don't think she was expecting to find you here or she'd have slowed down. It looked more like she was out on a general recon."

"D.C. must be getting desperate," Mac said. "He or she's been after me for nine days. If I don't get sprayed soon, he or she's bound to be thrown out of the game."

"I don't know why you keep saying 'he or she,'" Shell said. "If that was D.C., it's definitely a woman."

Mac didn't reply. His face was flushed, Shell saw. Maybe kissing him had been a mistake.

"I'm sorry if I embarrassed you," she told him. "Thing is, I've seen people do that in the movies and it always seems to work."

"I know what you mean," Mac said. "Playing this game, I often feel like I'm in a movie. That's part of the thrill, isn't it?"

He showed no sign of wanting to kiss her again.

GREEN

Jenny got into the Cartoonist's apartment building easily, by pretending to be the daughter of a tenant who was hard of hearing. An oldish lady on the way out let her in. Green tried a similar ruse. He pretended to be a computer technician who was there to help a deaf man reboot his computer. But his story didn't work on anyone coming out.

"Can't you e-mail or text him that you're waiting downstairs?"

"Sorry, this building has a very strict security code."

"Can I see your ID? This says you work over at the City Academy. What are you doing making house calls?"

"What deaf person? I'm on the building's social committee and I don't recall anybody with hearing problems on any of the floors."

"Um, I guess he's shy about it," Green told the last speaker. "Why don't I e-mail him?" He retreated to a park bench nearby. At least this would give him a good view if Drizzabone came after him.

Jenny phoned. She was setting up Green's laptop in an alcove near the Cartoonist's apartment.

"There are several surveillance cameras around, but I seem to be in a dead spot."

"Think you could come down and pretend to be going out, then let me in?"

"Not really. They have a camera on the door. It'd look really suspicious. You'll find a way. Be patient. I've found the Cartoonist's wi-fi signal, but I can't work out his password. Any ideas?"

"Hang on." Green had a second laptop, borrowed from work. He found an unsecured wireless network which he tapped into. Then he spoke to Jenny again. "I want you to let me into your laptop by remote access."

Once she did this, Green could see her computer, through which he could locate the Cartoonist's network. Cracking the wi-fi password shouldn't be hard. The night before, Green had researched the Cartoonist's life and work over the Net. In real life, the guy was pretty famous. Green knew the names of his parents, his ex-wife, his pet fish, and his one son. He tried them all. None worked.

Green kept at it. Maybe the guy actually did what everyone was supposed to do but hardly anybody did: used numbers as well as letters in his password. Green tried a thousand combinations, two thousand, three thousand, ten thousand . . . good thing he had a program to generate the passwords for him, or he'd be here all day.

"Everything all right?"

The guy standing by him wore overalls that looked too hot for the scorching day. He had brown hair and film star features.

"Eh, yeah, sure," Green said. A second sense sounded as the guy sat down next to him. This guy was a game player, no doubt about it. But no way was he Drizzabone, either, not unless he was a master of disguise and had just had his tattoo surgically removed.

"You want some help getting into that building?"

The gray light on the top right of Green's Macbook turned dark black. The last password had made a connection. He could use his target's broadband. Now Green had to find the Cartoonist's computer password. Once he had that, he would be able to find out everything about him. And he wanted the Cartoonist to know that.

"I do," he said. "Can you help me?"

"Depends," the newcomer said. "Are you playing the Spray game?"

"Sure am."

"I'll help you get in if you help me get my next target."

"Are they in the building, too?" Green asked.

"Not at the moment, but they will be."

"You've got a deal. I'm Green."

"People call me Lol."

Second Wednesday 11:47 A.M.
SHELL

When she got back to the dorm, Shell found that Cliff and Maiko were already there. The situation was as she'd suspected. Earlier, Maiko had turned up on time to relieve Cliff. The Invisible Man showed no signs of being home. Cliff persuaded Maiko to go back home with him. There, Cliff talked Maiko into joining him in a new game.

"You must have read about water war," Maiko told Shell. "Lots of people who were in the Spray game are playing. You have to join us."

"I promised I'd help Mac out. So did you."

"Not exactly. Helping him was your idea."

"If you say so," Shell said. "You and Cliff will still help us trap the Invisible Man after the lecture tomorrow, won't you?"

"Of course."

"Great. So why don't you tell me about this water war game?"

"It's a huge battle. Two teams, in the park, a week from Saturday. People wear different colored wrist bands, to show which sides they're on. Do you want to join us?"

"I'll think about it." That weekend, Mac might be in the final of the Spray game. The water war sounded like fun, but Shell's first loyalty was to him. On the other hand, if she didn't play, she'd be sending a clear signal to Cliff: She was more interested in some burger joint loser than she was in him. And she did like Cliff. He would still be around when the game was over. Mac wouldn't.

GREEN

The Cartoonist's password turned out to be an unlucky number added to the name of a famous Austrian cartoonist, Brick13. Once Green worked it out, his new friend said he knew how to get them both into the building.

"It's all a matter of charm," Lol told Green.

Lol had a toolbox with him. Standing by the entrance, he waved it at a woman who was leaving with a baby. She seemed distracted but not so distracted that she didn't get a good eyeful of Lol on her way out. What they said about the good looking was true, Green realized. They had special privileges.

"I don't suppose you're plumbers," the woman with the baby said, as Green held the door open for her. "The water pressure in the building is very low. I could barely take a shower this morning."

"Same all over the city," Green assured her. "Nothing to do with the plumbing."

Once they were in, he phoned Jenny. "I'm on my way up. Be ready to switch places with me in the alcove."

"Okay," Jenny said. "I'm ready."

"Sounds like you've got a plan worked out," Lol told Green.

"I'm still worried the Cartoonist will find Jenny before I have time to get upstairs with my weapon," Green told him.

"What are you using, a Destroyer?"

"Nah, I like those, but for an inside job like this, I really like the Flash Flood."

"Good choice. Want any help up there?"

"Better not. I'm conspicuous enough as it is. And my, uh . . . friend can distract the security cameras for me when she comes out of hiding."

"Okay. I'll wait outside so I don't raise any suspicions by hanging around here. But don't forget you promised to help me."

"I never break a promise, dude," Green said as he got into the elevator. "Whatever you need."

In the Cartoonist's corridor, Green found the alcove where Jenny had set up. She was crouched by a tiny window. There was no room for Green there as well, so they swapped places and laptops.

"He's definitely in?"

"Oh yes," Jenny said. "Look at the screen. He's accessing his e-mail at the moment."

"Okay," Green said. "Time for him to notice us."

As Jenny took off her sweatshirt, Green accessed the Cartoonist's bank account. Pity he couldn't access the Cartoonist's computer keychain for the password. The bank's security system wouldn't let the computer save it. Green turned this to his advantage. He had several attempts at the password, which was bound to set off an alarm of some kind.

"Okay," he told Jenny. "Go ahead."

Jenny took the backup laptop and crouched in the corridor, directly outside the Cartoonist's apartment. There was a security camera at the end of the hallway. The sight of a girl in an orange bikini, pretending to type, was bound to rouse even the sleepiest security guard. Green hoped the Cartoonist would be alerted first. On the screen, a message came up from the guy's bank.

> Your security is important to us. If your next attempt to access your account uses an incorrect password, your account will be frozen. You will not be able to access your account until you have reset your password by telephone. Do you want to continue?

Green paused. An e-mail would have been sent to the Cartoonist by now, asking him to confirm that he was trying to access his own account. All Green needed was for the Cartoonist to realize that his wi-fi was being leeched from close by. So he needed to create a connection problem. Green loaded an illegal BitTorrent site. He typed in the name of the most popular newly released movie and selected the version with the largest file size. It had hundreds of seeders, which would make the download quick, as fast as the Cartoonist's bandwidth would allow. Green clicked on *download*.

Megabytes poured into and out of his computer. If the Cartoonist was online, he would notice his connection speed slowing down to a trickle, like the water in Green's tap that morning. Come on! This was supposed to be a smart guy.

"Hey!"

Jenny gave a little screech. It was happening. Green pulled out his Flash Flood gun, which was primed and fully loaded.

He heard the Cartoonist's voice and recognized it at once. This guy was a famous TV personality, a game show host. And he wasn't alone.

"Move away from that laptop," the Cartoonist said. "For all I know, you might have a water balloon concealed in it."

"Whatever you say," Jenny said.

"Are you my assassin?" the TV personality asked. "Or a thief?"

"Neither," Jenny said. She took another step back. The Cartoonist picked up her laptop, examined it, then closed the lid. He put it down to one side. That was good. It belonged to the Academy and Green would rather not get it wet. Green moved out of the alcove into the corridor. The target had his back to him. Green stepped forward.

"Why are you dressed like that?" the Cartoonist asked Jenny.

"Because I wanted you to know that I wasn't carrying," Jenny said as something poked out from the Cartoonist's door. "And because I knew that I was going to get wet," she added.

Jenny hadn't noticed the mike yet, but Green could guess what was going on. TV personalities didn't play street games unless there was something in it for them. And they didn't have TV cameras in their homes unless they were participating in a reality TV show. Green nodded at his partner. Jenny glanced at Green in an obvious enough way for the Cartoonist to sense that something was wrong. As Green raised his Flash Flood, his target looked back over his shoulder. Too late. Green pressed the trigger. Water bounced off the guy's expensive hairpiece, covering his glasses and soaking his T-shirt.

"Come on!" Green called to Jenny. "He's making a TV show.

Let's get out of here before they show the whole world what we look like!"

Jenny picked up the laptop. Green kicked the Cartoonist's door back so that the cameras wouldn't get a good look at him.

"Your laminate," Green said in a stern voice.

"Oh, you're good," the TV star answered. "A glamorous girl in a bikini to distract me. That's very smart."

"It was her idea," Green said, taking the target laminate.

"How about an interview?" called a voice from behind the door.

"Not until this is over," Green said. "And don't follow me, or I'll soak all of your equipment, I swear!"

 Second Wednesday 12:11 P.M.
HAN

Han waited on D.C.'s block. There was only a slim chance the bike messenger would return here, but she had to take it. Han wished she were old enough to drive, that she could wait in a car, maybe pull up alongside D.C. at some traffic light, spray her on the road. Taxis were expensive, and buses gave you no flexibility.

D.C. didn't return. Han observed a couple of people using bike lockers. These were over on the side of the building that was farthest from the river. Now Han knew where D.C. was most likely keeping her bike. It should be only a matter of waiting. Sooner or later, she would be in a position to spray her. If D.C. ever came home.

The simplest way to stay safe in this game was to visit your home as little as possible. Han hadn't been back to her squat since Monday. Instead, she'd gone back to her real home. Mom thought camp was over. Tonight Han was supposed to be sleeping over at the house of a friend who would cover for her.

The idea came to Han out of the blue, the way the best ideas often do. D.C. was hard to track down because she had a vehicle that could go anywhere, that was flexible and not confined to any traffic system. Last night, Han had borrowed Mom's backup credit card to use in an emergency. Now was the time to use it.

Second Wednesday 12:13 P.M.
GREEN

"Did you recognize him?" Green asked Jenny on the elevator down. Green was so excited, he wanted to hug Jenny but didn't have the nerve. "That isn't his real name on the laminate."

"Maybe it is," Jenny said. "TV people have made-up names, stage names. Green isn't your real name, is it?"

"Maybe it is. Maybe it isn't. Is Jenny your real name?"

"Nothing about me's real," Jenny told him.

He didn't know how to reply to her. They ought to be celebrating, not discussing the ins and outs of pseudonyms.

"Oh, I forgot," he said. "There's this guy downstairs waiting for us. He helped me to get in. So I said we'd help him with his next kill."

"I'll bet you did," Jenny muttered.

"What's going on, Jenny? We just pulled off a superb hit. It'll be on TV. Even if I don't win, we'll be stars."

"It wasn't part of my plan," Jenny said. "And I like you, Green. That wasn't part of my plan, either."

They stepped out of the elevator.

"There he is," Green said. Lol was standing on the other side of the glass doors. Green worried. How could he hope to win a girl like Jenny when there was a guy as handsome as Lol around? He glanced at Jenny to see how she reacted to Lol, but she was looking at the elevator display. Another car was on its way down.

"That'll be the TV crew," Green said. "Let's get out of here!"

"Don't you want to be famous?" Jenny asked. "You stay in here. I'll go and help this Lol guy."

"What's going on?" Green asked her. Full of adrenaline, he plucked the courage to ask her what was on his mind. "Am I missing something here? Don't you want to be seen with me?"

"It's not that. I like you. A lot. It's just . . ." Lol rapped on the glass door, indicating that they should come out. There was a bulge in the side of his overalls. Of course, he was packing.

Jenny spoke in a rush. "Listen, Green. I already have a boy-friend. Him, out there. His real name's Lawrence and his game ID is Lol. Lol's your assassin, not Drizzabone. When Lol was given you as a target, he got me to pretend I was a player and that you were my target. He even made up Drizzabone, put stuff about him on the game Web site. The idea was that I would find out if you had a difficult target, then lead Lol to you when you got an easy one."

"How could you?" Green asked. He felt disgusted with her and even more disgusted with himself, for trusting her.

"Lol's very persuasive. I thought it was just a game. Now I see how seriously you take it. I like you, Green, I don't want to hurt you. So stay, be interviewed. I'll try and get rid of Lol, for now at least. . . ."

The elevator door rang. The TV crew stepped out.

"Stay with me," Green asked Jenny. "Help me win."

"How?" Jenny asked, her voice plaintive, pained.

Green shouted to the crew. "Okay, I'll do your interview. But before you do me, you really have to talk to that guy outside. He's the legendary Zorro. I was with him on his very first hit, when he took out a City Academy student called Maiko in the first minute of the game. You'd be crazy not to interview him first!"

The crew, all six of them, charged out of the building, surrounding Lol.

"What's it going to be?" Green asked Jenny. "Are you staying with him, or coming with me?"

Mac and Shell hung around the corridor outside the lecture hall watching as students straggled inside.

"This is so dangerous," Shell told Mac. "Suppose your assassin's in there? You've no idea what she looks like."

"I suppose D.C. could be a student, but the chances of her knowing about this seminar are fairly low."

"You say that, but a lot of people have gone in already."

"Not our Invisible Man, though."

Mac's target hadn't stayed at his own house the night before. He and Shell had borrowed Cliff's car and watched until two. Today, if the Invisible Man was around, he hadn't approached his office from the most obvious entrance. But the campus was a maze of buildings. This was going to be even more difficult than he'd feared.

A guy walked past, in typical student garb: jeans, sneakers, a plain T-shirt. There was something familiar about him. Probably a customer from the burger bar. The guy went into the lecture hall.

"We might as well go in now," Shell said.

"You're sure nobody will know I'm not a student?"

"Believe me, you look the part."

The room was nearly full. The Invisible Man strode to the podium at exactly 1:30, the lecture's start time. The Invisible

Man's hair was cropped so close, it was hard to tell where his bald patch started and his real hair ended. He had a jutting jaw and wide, lively eyes. Beneath his sports jacket, he wore a pink, collarless shirt.

"'Whiskey is for drinking, water is for fighting over.' Mark Twain said that in 1881, but it's never been more true than it is today. Clean water is at a premium. You only have to look at the trickle of water coming through your taps. Water shortages bring disease, poverty, and untold environmental damage. Rivers run through more than one country and when one country tries to divert a river, or build a dam that stops the water from reaching another country, wars break out. In the last 50 years, there have been over 500 conflicts between countries with 21 instances of actual hostilities, as a result of disagreements over water. All of which puts in perspective the hose bans and four-minute showers the government is telling us to take. And it trivializes what I'm here to talk to you about today...."

Suddenly, the Invisible Man opened his jacket to reveal a leather holster beneath his left shoulder. He brandished a slender black revolver. The audience gasped. They weren't used to seeing guns on campus. But Mac recognized the model at once. It was an old-school water pistol with a reloadable water magazine. The Invisible Man pressed the trigger and a jet of water crossed the room. The Invisible Man sprayed a no-cell-phone sign on the far wall. It was a flashy, empty gesture. You weren't allowed to use realistic guns in the Spray game, for fear of panic on the streets. But the Invisible Man had his audience's attention. As the water dripped onto the lecture hall's tiled floor, there was some laughter and scattered applause. The Invisible Man warmed to his theme.

"Water is at the heart of our existence. We can't live without it. It covers four fifths of our planet, yet we are always running short of it. And today, I want to talk to you about two games that provide a choice of metaphors for the place of water in the world today. One is an assassination game. The other is all-out warfare. . . ."

 Second Thursday 1:34 P.M.
JENNY

"I don't know what I'm doing here," Jenny told Green as they jumped onto the bus. "Lol's my boyfriend. We've been going out for two months."

"Get off and go back to him if you want," Green said, but it was already too late. The bus was moving.

Jenny didn't really want to get off. If she was honest with herself, looks aside, she liked Green much more than she liked Lol. Half the girls in her grade thought Lol was God's gift. Of course, when he asked her out, she said yes. When he asked for help in the Spray game, she did what he asked. Jenny was lucky to be with him, everyone said that. In the good-looking league, she was an eight out of ten. In good light, a nine. Lol was a nine verging on ten.

"You saved me," Green said. "I appreciate it, no matter what you did before."

"Lol could have sprayed you two days ago," Jenny told him. "But then I told him your new target was the Cartoonist and you had a better chance of spraying him than he did. Lol could never have pulled off a stunt like the one we just did. But he'd have done the assassination himself if he'd known the target was a celebrity. Lol really wants to be famous. He figures, with his looks, it's only a matter of time before some big TV deal comes knocking at his door. Winning the game would speed that up."

"He just got his TV interview," Green pointed out.

"I wouldn't put it past Lol to pretend he is Zorro," Jenny said with a smirk. "Except, doesn't Zorro have a mustache?"

"A minor inconvenience," Green said. "But I've met Zorro. He seemed like a nice guy to me. This Lol guy sounds like a user. So how come you're still going out with him?"

Jenny didn't know how to answer this. "Seems I'm not, anymore. He's bound to dump me when he realizes I told you who he was."

"Not if you dump him first."

"You've got a point." Jenny got out her phone and texted Lol. *Consider yourself dumped, loser!* It felt good. She wouldn't miss him. But she'd miss the envious looks of other girls when she was out with him. What would those girls say if they saw her out with Green? He was clever, and considerate, and funny, and cuddly. It would be a stretch to call him handsome, but his face had character.

"Who's on the Cartoonist's target laminate?" she asked Green.

"I haven't had a chance to look yet." He got it out. "Uh-oh."

"What is it?" Jenny asked with a sinking feeling. "Someone you've heard of?"

"I knew I shouldn't have invoked his name earlier," Green said, handing her the card. The photo on it was of a long-haired man with a pencil mustache. Zorro.

Second Thursday 2:13 P.M.
MAC

"The basic aim of a water war is to get your opponents as wet as possible. The game can be played by a huge number of people in a variety of ways—one-hit kills, free-for-all, as a kind of tag. But a general principle holds: The side with the most dry members at the end is the one that wins. Water war resembles real warfare, with water substituting for blood.

"The world is short of water, but we would rather waste a small amount of water than spill a lot of blood. If only governments could agree to settle real wars with water pistols, think how many lives could be saved! Unfortunately, as we have already discussed, water is more likely to be the cause of wars than it is to be the solution.

"The other game, the one that I'm involved in at the moment, is known as Killer, Street Wars, or, more poetically, Spray. Historically, it derives from a game called Assassins. This game is all about the individual. It's thought that Assassins was first played in schools, although the variant involving water weapons is more recent.

"Spray is a game designed by and for individuals. Some versions allow teamwork but the rules always specify that the team has to have a leader and if that leader is assassinated, the whole team is out. So it's really about individuals with a support network rather than a team. It's a very pure game, a competition that can have only one winner. It's a game that encourages deviousness, selfishness, and, most of all, ingenuity. I'm writing a book about its history. But that's not my main motive for joining the game this year. My main motive, and that of the other players, is not to win. It's to have fun."

There was mild applause, which the lecturer waved aside. "We have time for a few questions."

"How many people have you killed?" a girl at the front wanted to know.

"Four. That's one more than the average for people who've got this far in the game. Experience shows that anybody who doesn't have three hits by tomorrow will be eliminated from the game."

"Who runs the game?"

"Somebody who calls himself the gamekeeper. At least, the person I met looked like a he. And the gamekeeper has assistants. There's some debate about whether it's always the same person throughout the game or whether the mantle of gamekeeper is passed on. I don't think this matters too much. The only thing is that, whoever takes over the role has to have independent means. The game's entry fees are low. The prize isn't very high, either, but there must be a lot of expenses."

"What's your name in this game?"

"I call myself the Invisible Man after the book by H. G. Wells, meaning that I hope not to be spotted. Although, giving a talk like this hardly helps my invisibility."

There were polite chuckles. *Can't be many jokes during lectures,* Mac figured, *if they think that's funny.* Shell waved her arm in the air and was called.

"Do you think your assassin is in the audience?" she asked.

"More than likely, but I've no way of knowing who my assassin is, until they spray me with a water pistol or soak me with a water balloon. At least I know that they can't get me in here. The rules are very clear. You can't soak a person in their workplace—or their home, unless the target is foolish enough to invite the assassin inside."

"Are you in this game to win?" Mac asked, worried that his voice would not seem as educated as the others in the room.

"There's no point in playing a game you don't intend to win," the Invisible Man answered. "But the favorite has to be a player who calls himself Zorro. He's won twice before. What he does is he moves to the game cities in order to qualify for the competition. He's very devious. He took out a student on this very campus in the first minute of the game."

The Invisible Man described the double bluff that Zorro had used to take out Cliff and Maiko. There was more laughter; then the Invisible Man looked at his watch. He pointed at a display on the digital whiteboard.

"Follow the game on the Web site shown here if you're interested. And you can observe or even participate in the water war at the city park a week from Saturday. It's rare that you get two games going on at the same time, so make the most of it. Presuming, that is, you can get hold of enough water to fill your pistols."

He grinned, then slammed a new magazine into his water pistol and took aim at the rear door.

"Remember, don't use realistic pistols like this on the street. They could easily raise a panic. Now, who dares leave first?"

Second Friday 2:37 P.M.
GREEN

Jenny and Green went for a swim at the crowded public pool, then returned to Green's one-bedroom apartment. He lived on a narrow street not far from campus. Luckily, the place wasn't too big a mess.

"I can't take out Zorro!" Green moaned. He put on a German accent. "For me, the war is over."

"Have more faith in yourself," Jenny said. "It's better to have Zorro as your target than to have him as your assassin. You know who your assassin is, and he's no great shakes. I can help protect you from him."

Green looked at the laminate again. It told him Zorro's real name and address. His target even had a job, though Green doubted he'd be there much. According to the laminate, Zorro was a systems analyst. His address was in one of the cheapest parts of the city—an area full of squats and derelict housing. It made for a good fake address. And a dangerous hunting ground.

"Didn't you meet him on day one?" Jenny asked. "At least you know what he looks like."

She looked distracted. It was probably sinking in that she'd just dumped her handsome bastard of a boyfriend to hook up with a bloated porpoise. Green mustn't let himself get too taken with Jenny. He'd had crushes on girls before. Friendship soon turned to pity if he showed an unexpected romantic side. Embarrassment all around.

"According to the laminate, Zorro lives over on the west side," he said. "Public transportation's terrible in that part of the city. Even with a taxi, we'll be vulnerable to Lol as soon as we get out onto the street."

"One thing about Lol," Jenny said. "He's too lazy to learn to drive."

"Unfortunately," Green said, "the same thing goes for me."

"But not me," Jenny said. "I passed my test last month. Want to see if I can borrow my mom's car?"

MAC

Mac and Shell lingered in the gray corridor outside the lecture hall, waiting for the Invisible Man to leave. Shell pretended to read a bulletin board. The guy who Mac had half recognized on the way in brushed past them on his way out. Something made Mac say hello.

"How're you doing?" the guy responded, as though he knew who Mac was.

"Okay. What did you think of the lecture?"

"Pretty basic stuff. But that's school for you. They're always years behind the time but like to think they're cutting edge." He lowered his voice. "Is he your target?"

Mac nodded.

"Have you got a plan to get him?"

"Not really," Mac said. "He's pretty safe here."

"Only while he's inside," the guy pointed out. "You never know, he might fall for the old fire alarm trick. If you were a student here, that would get you into trouble, but ... here he comes."

Mac saw his chance.

"Who was that guy you were talking to?" Shell asked.

"I think he's another player," Mac told her. "He gave me an idea. See that cluster of people around the Invisible Man? I want you to join them and ..."

He lowered his voice. Shell listened, then hurried off to join the lecturer. The guy who had offered Mac the advice was already at the stairs. How did he know that Mac wasn't a student? The guy needed a haircut. His heavy black-rimmed glasses made it hard to get a good look at his face. Even so, Mac recognized him. He knew that voice. Of course. That was who he was! No wonder he was here.

The gamekeeper nodded to Mac before turning away. Mac gave him a half smile in return. Then he broke the glass on the fire alarm.

Second Friday 2:46 P.M.
HAN

Han's new bike was highly weaponized. She had a water mortar on the back panel. It held half a dozen water balloons, any one of which could soak a target. She had a Super Soaker clipped to the crossbar, where she could grab it and aim at a moment's notice. And she had a purple double helix blaster strapped to her back, resting against her right shoulder. This was a big gun that didn't need pressurizing and had a decent range. Oh yes, Han was well prepared. All she had to do was locate her target.

Han wanted to eliminate D.C. before the weekend was over. Otherwise, she knew, the target might change. D.C. had made only one kill, on the first day. If she was going to get another by tomorrow night, she would have to move quickly. The way Han saw it, D.C. must have been given a very difficult target. This close to the wire, she was bound to take risks to get her or him. Risks that exposed her.

Han had another target, too. She must have shown Chris's photo to a thousand people. One or two recognized him. A couple said he had served them in a bar. One claimed he worked in a restaurant. No solid details.

Three people—each a student—reckoned he'd served them a burger, though none was certain where. Han had twice toured the fast food places around the City Academy, with no sign of Chris. This afternoon, short of other ideas, she decided to go into them one more time.

She got lucky on her third stop. A guy named Ben.

"Looks like an old photo of my friend Mac. He worked here until a few days ago."

"He did? Why did he leave?"

"You're in the game, right?"

"Uh, yeah."

"And that's your bike outside?"

"Yes."

"You look smaller than you do on the bike, but it's you, D.C.?"

"Oh. No." Han didn't know what to say. She'd struck lucky. D.C. was her target. Mac was D.C.'s target. She was only one kill away from him. "I'm not her."

"Then how do you know it's a her, huh? Mac wasn't sure."

"Because . . . look, I'm an old friend of his. Do you have an address, or a phone number?"

"Don't they give you that info on the target laminate?"

"They do. But he's not my target, honest. He's . . ."

She almost said "my brother" but stopped herself.

"Thing is," Ben said, "I promised Mac I wouldn't give anyone any info about him. He's got this grungy little apartment but it wouldn't help you to know where it is, because he's never there."

"Never?"

"Are you sure you're not his assassin?"

"No. Of course not." Han got out her target laminate and showed it to Ben. "See? I'm after the person who's after him."

Ben still didn't look convinced. "You look a little young to be playing the game. Isn't it for fifteen and over?"

"I am fifteen," Han insisted. "And a half," she added, feeling foolish as the words came out. Ben didn't look convinced. In daylight, without makeup, Han barely looked her real age, which was fourteen.

"And you say you're an old friend of Mac's?"

"That's right," Han said.

"Tell you what. I get off at eight tonight. Meet me for a drink and I'll give Mac a call, see if he's willing to meet you."

"Great. Where?"

They picked a café to meet in. Han wasn't sure she'd make it. She'd found out three things: 1. Chris was calling himself Mac. 2. He was still in the game, and 3. His assassin was D.C. If Han got to D.C. she would get to Chris. She had to find her this afternoon. She had to.

SHELL

Shell knew two things about fire alarms. The first was that, when a fire alarm sounded, everybody was supposed to go to a specific place. The second was that nobody ever knew where that specific place was. As the alarm screeched, deafeningly, through the echoey corridors, people scattered in different directions. The Invisible Man still had a crowd of students around him, including Shell. She glanced in the direction that she had last seen Mac, but he wasn't there. Which was good. Mac had to follow the Invisible Man outside, but not too obviously. The Invisible Man mustn't spot him. If necessary, Shell could always call Mac to let him know where his target was standing.

"Which way?" she asked the Invisible Man, who was grinning as though he had set off the fire alarm himself. He consulted a sign.

"Follow me!" he called. The Invisible Man guided Shell and a group of students down a stairwell. At the bottom was an exit that opened into a loading area. The Invisible Man held the door open for his fan club.

Shell contrived to be the last one out. As she went through the door, she turned to thank the lecturer. But he was already slipping away, heading back toward where he'd come from.

"Hey!" she said. "You can't go back in there."

He gave her a sly grin. "I'm the Invisible Man. I have to disappear."

Shell tried to stall him. "Doesn't it show more skill to disappear outside than it does in here, where nobody's allowed to spray you?"

"Good point, but—" The lecturer was interrupted by what appeared to be a security guard, in his distinctive green, short-sleeved shirt.

"Everyone outside, please. No exceptions. Outside. Now!"

"Show me your bag, would you?" the Invisible Man asked Shell. "I just want to be sure you're not my assassin."

"If you don't mind, sir, I need you outside now!" The security guard was younger than the retired police officers who usually did the job, but he had the polite yet firm manner down pat. The Invisible Man didn't challenge him. Having seen that Shell wasn't carrying, the lecturer allowed the security guard to herd him outside. In the hot air, he nervously scanned their surroundings, looking for any sign of his assassin.

"Would you like me to escort you to your car, sir?" the security officer asked.

"That won't be necessary," the Invisible Man said. "If you could just tell me how far I am from the main entrance parking lot."

"Certainly, sir. Let me show you on this map."

As Mac reached into his capacious pockets, the Invisible Man appeared to notice that the guard's loose, gray trousers didn't match his shirt. Shell had been wondering how long it would take him to catch on. Too long. There was no time for him to run. Mac already had the water pistol in his hand.

"You devious . . ."

Mac sprayed the guy's pink, collarless shirt, the water hitting so hard that the hairs in the lecturer's chest showed through the thin fabric.

"Enough, enough!" A few of the students from the lecture were still around. Moments ago, they had been hanging on the lecturer's every word. Now they looked back and giggled.

"Your laminate, please," Mac said.

"That was so cool," Shell told him. "Where did you get that shirt and clipboard?"

"The storage closet I ducked into after sounding the alarm."

"The school will not look kindly on your behavior this afternoon," the lecturer told Mac, handing him his card.

"What makes you think I'm a student?" Mac said, taking off his security guard shirt and throwing it to the ground.

Second Saturday 9:02 A.M.
HAN

GAMEKEEPER COMMUNIQUE NUMBER 2
Return-Path: <gamekeeper@assassins.org.uk>
Received: from aamtain07-winn.ispmail.nodoby.com
([81.103.221.35])
for <addresslist concealed>; 76:00:36 +0800

Eleven days gone and the final week is almost upon us. Most of you receiving this are serious players with three or four kills under your belt. Some have significantly more. Time to get down to the nitty-gritty. If you don't have three kills by midnight tonight, I don't care how tough your target is, you're out. Keep your laminate as a souvenir—there'll be new ones for the players who make it through to the final week. They can expect an e-mail tomorrow.

Han closed her e-mail and looked out of the train window. She had no idea who her new assassin was. That Academy student came close but not close enough, and Han had avoided the squat since then. Last night, Han had gone home, and now she was taking the train back into the city. Mom thought she was out on a shopping day. Mom was easy to fool, mainly because she was home so little herself.

Yesterday, Han had wasted the whole day searching for her target. Last night, she'd stood up Ben. She'd thought the scenario through and meeting him wouldn't work. Before he gave out her brother's address, Ben was bound to call Chris. He'd put Han on the line. That wasn't how she wanted to encounter him, not after all these years. Suppose he rejected her, refused to meet? No. Han wanted to meet Chris face-to-face, without warning.

D.C. should have received the same e-mail from the game-keeper. She would be after Mac, as Chris called himself. Han hoped to get to her before she left her apartment. But if she couldn't it didn't matter much. Yesterday, before she went home, Han had broken into D.C.'s bike locker. She didn't take anything. But she did leave something behind.

Shell and Mac ate a late breakfast in the dorm's small kitchen. Outside, the sky was a steely blue. It was going to be another hot one.

"Why do you keep looking outside?" Shell asked.

"I keep expecting to see a cyclist coming for me. D.C. has to get me today, or be eliminated."

"Maybe you're being paranoid," Shell said. "Could be D.C.'s given up. She's waiting to be eliminated from the game. So you need to worry about tomorrow. When you get a new assassin."

"There can't be that many players left," Mac said. "With my luck, I'll get Zorro."

Shell examined Mac's new target laminate.

"This one doesn't sound too difficult."

"Everybody's difficult at this stage. If a player's lasted this long, they have to be good."

"Yes," Shell said. "But you're better."

"No, I'm just lucky. If I hadn't met you . . ."

He looked at her and Shell beamed at him. Maybe this was the moment when he'd say something romantic. She'd spent ages brushing her hair this morning, chosen her most flattering clothes, even though she was likely to get soaked. But Mac seemed not to notice. There had been no follow-up to their kiss, which was days ago. He seemed immune to physical attraction.

He wasn't gay. She'd never seen him glance at a guy with a flicker of interest. Maybe he was a late developer. Or it could be he already had a girlfriend, hiding in his mysterious past.

A week ago, Shell could have had Cliff, who she half crushed on. But he was with Maiko now. And who could blame him for picking her? Shell had made her interest in Mac clear. But she'd made the wrong choice.

"Have you got your Super Soaker ready?" she asked Mac.

"Primed for action," he said, glancing once more at the laminate before putting it in his wallet. "Let's go."

Second Saturday 11:21 A.M.

HAN

D.C. was on the move again. Han watched on her laptop as she navigated her way across the city. Han had chosen the café she was sitting in because it was a central location. If D.C. took an obvious route, Han might be able to intercept her. You could really zip around on a bicycle.

The GPS device Han had hidden under D.C.'s rear mud-guard was the one Mom had planted on the car of her second husband when he was playing around. The day he left home, there was no note, only the round metal tracker on the table in the hall. Han had taken it.

That day, she'd shown Mom the tracker and told her not to even think about keeping tabs on her the same way. Han was all Mom had left, so she'd given her all kinds of freedom, not checking up on her when she pretended to be staying with friends, or gone off on unannounced trips. This evening, if Han hadn't sprayed D.C. by then, she'd go out with a fictitious friend, whose home she'd stay in overnight.

Was D.C. stalking Chris, or making bike deliveries? She went past the same place twice, stopping for five minutes each time. Han took a note of the approximate address. It could be where Chris lived.

Han was paranoid that her own assassin would be getting as busy as she was. He or she had been on the job for six days. Han had only been back to the apartment once in that time. She could be reported for breaking the rules. But she had read through the archived messages of previous tournaments. Players didn't tend to be thrown out for breaking residency rules. Other rules, yes, including the one about age. That could disqualify her at any time.

D.C. had been stopped at the Academy campus for more than five minutes. Not too far to ride. Han paid for her coffee and slid her laptop into her backpack, where it nestled next to her reserve Super Soaker. She put on her white face mask. More and more people were wearing these because of pollution and super-bugs. Together with the cycle helmet, it did a really good job of disguising her.

MAC

Mac felt conspicuous walking around with a Super Soaker in his hand. Shell, similarly armed, was to his left, Maiko to his right. Most guys would pay a small fortune to have two such attractive, older women as their entourage. But Mac wasn't most guys. He was in this city to win, not to get a girlfriend.

"Look out!" Shell said. "Behind you!"

Maiko was supposed to be watching the rear. Mac swiveled around, but it was too late. A torrent of brackish water sprayed him, soaking his T-shirt, trickling down into his jeans. He swore.

"This water's filthy! You're supposed to use clean!"

"It's recycled water," Cliff explained. "If we'd tried to fill the Super Soakers from taps, we'd have been there all day. The pressure's way down again."

"We managed to fill ours!" Maiko said, pushing the shaft of her double helix gun so that it pummeled a picturesque spray at Cliff.

"I'll get you back!" Cliff insisted, pointing his Super Soaker at her. But he had used most of his water already and had forgotten to pump the pressure back up. All that came out was a pitiful stream. The spray dribbled to the dry ground before it could reach Maiko.

Cliff and Maiko were practicing for the water war. It gave them an excuse to use the Super Soakers they'd bought two weeks earlier. Was it less than two weeks since the game began? It felt longer to Shell. Two weeks ago, she didn't know that Mac existed. Now she was, at most, a week away from losing him.

"Isn't this more fun than an assassination game?" Cliff asked Mac. Both of them were dripping wet but looked happy.

"I prefer games that have winners and losers," Mac said. "In this game, everybody gets wet."

As if to prove his point, a bunch of male students charged onto the lawn. They carried a variety of water weapons and were whooping like they were at a concert or a big game. One of them saw the two dry girls with the two wet boys. He aimed his CPS.

"Look out!" Shell called. She got behind the two boys, who took the brunt of the spray aimed at her. Maiko wasn't so lucky. She was soaked from head to toe. The group of guys ran off laughing. Shell aimed a torrent at the one who had shot at her and Maiko, but only caught him on the shoulder.

"We'll get you next Saturday!" Cliff yelled at them, then turned to the others. "I'm going to reload."

"I'm going to get changed," Maiko said. "Back in five."

Shell looked at Mac. He seemed distracted.

"What's wrong?" she asked him. "Want to go in and put on some dry stuff? Cliff could lend you some clothes."

"No thanks," Mac said. "I'll dry off soon enough in this heat. I'm worried because there are so many cyclists on the path over there. It makes me nervous."

"You're out of range standing here. But maybe we should get after your target," Shell suggested.

"I told Cliff we'd hang with him and Maiko for an hour; then he's going to give us a lift."

"We could always catch a bus," Shell said.

"I'd feel more comfortable in a car. You're more in control."

"How did you plan to play this game before you met us?" Shell asked.

"On foot, if necessary. But this is more fun." He gave her a wry smile. "You ought to refill your Super Soaker."

"I don't think so," Shell said. "We're wasting time."

"It's only a game," Mac reminded her. "We're just passing the time. One game's as good as another for getting through the day."

Maiko returned, wearing a dry T-shirt. She waved at Cliff, who was trying to reload his weapon from the water fountain. The trickle of discolored liquid coming from the fountain was pitifully thin.

"Okay," Shell said. "Let's play."

 Second Saturday 11:38 A.M.
HAN

Han made good time across the city but not necessarily good enough. While cycling, she wasn't connected. She didn't know where D.C. was. Han would have to find a wi-fi hot spot before she could check the GPS she'd planted on D.C.'s bike. Earlier, she'd observed D.C. going back and forth in the part of the city she was entering now. This area was dominated by the City Academy, a private high school. Once, Han planned to go there. But the tuition became too expensive after Mom spent all the money Dad left her.

D.C. was unlikely to be on a delivery. She'd be stalking her target. If Han cycled around the same area, she might stumble upon her.

There was a big water fight next week. Han had seen posters for it. There were teenagers with water pistols everywhere, practicing. Heat wave foolishness. Still, their frantic activity provided Han with good cover.

Why was D.C. stalking Chris here? Surely he was too old to be at the Academy? That said, D.C. was clever enough to be in the right place. Han wouldn't put it past Chris to fake an ID. Maybe the real Mac was somebody whose identity Chris had stolen. That could be how he disappeared off the face of the earth so completely.

Han came to a large parking lot. Amazing how, in a city with a great public transportation network, so many high school kids had cars. You got around quicker on a bike. Today proved that. And cycling was healthier than driving. Messier, though. Han had been cycling frantically and the sweat was pouring down her back. Time to take off her mask and wipe her face, which was sticky and dirty and felt gross.

There she was! Han's target was stationary, at the edge of the car park, hidden behind a purple car. What was D.C. watching?

Han had no time to waste. She remounted her bike and

cycled down the next lane to the one where D.C. was waiting. Her Super Soaker was in position, fully primed. Chances were, she could spray her now, no trouble. But Han wanted to see D.C.'s target first. She wanted to see her brother.

MAC

Maiko, Shell, and Cliff escorted Mac to the car in classic entourage style: Cliff in front, with Shell and Maiko flanking Mac. Cars posed a special danger to Mac. An assassin could hide in one or behind one. Cliff's car was at the near end of the car park.

"Looks clear," Cliff said, scanning the people within range.

"How can you be sure?" Shell asked. "Mac's assassin might have changed twice since he was stalked by the cyclist. It could be that middle-aged guy over there, talking to a student. Or that girl behind the SUV, the one wearing a face mask."

"What girl?" Maiko asked. "I don't see her."

They reached Cliff's red Hyundai.

"Let's just get in the car," Mac said.

Cliff opened the driver's door and Shell opened the passenger door. She pushed the passenger seat down. This was the moment when Mac was most exposed. He had to clamber over the lowered seat to get in the back. Shell glanced at the girl in the face mask. For a moment, their eyes met. Then the girl looked away. Shell followed her gaze.

142

"Get down!" she told Mac, pushing him to the concrete floor.

Only sixty feet away from them stood D.C. The cyclist, in gray jeans and a T-shirt, was pointing a Super Soaker in Mac's direction. She was in range, but did she have a clear shot? Not if Shell and Maiko blocked Mac. Shell grabbed her friend. Both of them stood over Mac. D.C. hesitated. Was she going to try to come closer? Then something happened.

The spray of water was sudden, swift, and definitive. One moment D.C. was pointing her Super Soaker. The next she was drenched from head to toe, sparkling with water and shaking her head in order to see her assassin. That was when she took off her helmet. Now Shell could see that D.C. was definitely a woman in her mid-twenties. And she had been taken out by a girl. The other cyclist, the one in the face mask, who was approaching her, barely looked old enough to be in the game. But she was.

Cliff started the engine.

"You're safe," Shell told Mac, who was in the back of the car.

"Until the new assassin gets the laminate," Mac said. "Quick, get in! I want a look at her."

Shell joined Mac in the back. Maiko took the front passenger seat. Cliff began to drive in the direction of the wet woman cyclist.

"You two had me covered," Mac said. "Thanks."

They got close to where the girl was talking to the woman. Face Mask had her back to the car. She and D.C. were between two cars, so Shell couldn't see her properly. Cliff honked his horn, trying to get the new assassin to turn around. D.C. scowled at all three of them, then gave Cliff's windshield a blast with her Super Soaker. Face Mask glanced over her shoulder to see what was happening, but with her mask and helmet, it was hard to tell how much hair she had, never mind what her face looked like.

"I've swapped one dangerous cyclist for another," Mac said. "Come on, let's get out of here."

"She knows where I've been staying," Mac said, once they were on the main road. "I need a new hideout for the final week."

Shell's heart sank. This could be their last afternoon together.

 Second Saturday 11:45 A.M.
HAN

Blast! Han watched the red car leave the parking lot. It was too much to ask that she could get to Chris the same day she sprayed D.C. At least, now, she knew the car's license plate number and had gotten a good look at Chris's friends, who appeared to be Academy students. Her brother was her target now. She would track him down in good time, especially if she recovered her little gadget. D.C. stood up.

"Do you know how long I've been tracking him?" she asked Han. "Since the second day of the game. I nearly had him then. But he's really hard to catch."

"You were pretty tricky, too," Han said.

"You're a fool. If you'd waited a minute, until I sprayed him, then you'd have been given a new target, probably an easier one. Whereas now, Mac's seen you. He'll be even harder to catch."

"I'm no fool," Han said, reaching under the panel of D.C.'s bike and pulling out the little tracking device. "See?"

"You're resourceful, but you'll have trouble pinning that to him. He doesn't have a bike, or a car. Don't bother going to his apartment. He's never there. And he's quit his job."

"Then how did you find him?"

"He sprayed an Academy lecturer yesterday. There was loads of discussion about it on the game blogs. This kid called Cliff boasted that he'd been helping to hide Mac. I worked out that Cliff was a boarder at the City Academy, so I came looking." D.C. reached into her back pocket. "Here." She handed over the laminate.

"Thanks."

"Aren't you a little young to be playing this game?"

"Aren't you a little old?"

Han glanced at the details on the laminate. Not a word on there was true. Her brother was always really sneaky when it came to playing games.

GAMEKEEPER

And then there were nine.

The gamekeeper finished checking his e-mail. The midnight deadline had cleared the decks. There had been lots of frantic activity yesterday. Players eliminated all over the place. This morning, he had only had to send out three e-mails, removing players from the game. This meant he had to send just three e-mails assigning new targets. He would deliver the new target laminates shortly, for, at this stage of the game, every single hour was crucial.

Less than two weeks in, the game was down to single figures: 4.5 percent of the original entry. The game might not last a full third week. Hard to tell. Sometimes, this stage of the game lingered. The cagier players who remained took so many precautions that none of them was able to get near each other. Gridlock. If that happened, the gamekeeper had to engineer a final game shoot-out, sometimes with himself as the target. This time, however, by eliminating players without multiple hits, he had made such an outcome less likely. The gamekeeper tweaked the rules every time, improving the experience.

There were some very good players left. Zorro, as a past winner, had to be the favorite, but Green was sharp, for a first timer, and the mysterious Mac intrigued him. Then there was Han. His assistant said she might be underage, with a fake ID. But if you were clever enough to fake your way in, you were clever enough to play the game. Senile was the game's oldest player, although he might not be in the game for long, being Zorro's next target. The full target and assassin list looked like this:

Mac–Badmonkey
Badmonkey–Keno
Keno–Peg
Peg–Lol
Lol–Green
Green–Zorro
Zorro–Senile
Senile–Han
Han–Mac

Would these last players fall quickly? The contests he liked best were ones where there was a clear winner, without his intervention. Some juggling of targets was always required in the final week, to ensure that there was only one winner. But he had a hunch. This time, the game could be over by tomorrow evening.

GREEN

Green and Jenny sat in her car, watching the apartment where Zorro was supposed to be staying. There had been no sign of him since they showed up yesterday evening. Jenny had tried the door twice, with a convincing story at the ready. No response.

Green didn't mind. This was the first night he had spent alone with a girl. At ten, she'd phoned her parents, said she was staying at a friend's. Jenny was such a good liar. They'd stayed up all night, talking, then agreed to take turns to nap. Jenny dozed, her head resting on Green's shoulder. It felt intimate, comfortable. It felt right.

Someone turned onto the street and Green slid down his seat, jerking Jenny awake.

"Is it him?" she asked as a thin man crossed the street.

"I don't think so." Green had seen Zorro up close. He'd had a good look at his long hair and mustache and didn't think that they were fake. But this guy was the right age and build. He could have gotten a haircut and a shave.

"It could be him," Green said.

"Then don't take chances. Spray him!"

She was right. If the thin man went to the right building, Green would jump out of the car and . . . and . . .

Suppose it was a double bluff? Suppose Lol was watching their car and had sent a decoy over to draw them out? Lol knew Jenny's car. The thin man turned a corner, heading away from the building. Not Zorro.

"I'm thirsty," Jenny said. "The water bottle's empty."

They had been stuffed in this car for seventeen hours straight. They probably reeked. But Green felt great. Or, if not great, exactly, happy. He'd stay another seventeen hours, if that was what Jenny wanted. But if she wanted a drink, fine. This was only a game. He'd made it to the last week. He'd met Jenny. He was already a winner.

"He's not coming back," Green said. "That's presuming he lives here at all. Let's go back to my place for a shower and lunch."

"What about Lol?" Jenny said. "Won't he be waiting there?"

"With any luck, Lol is Zorro's target and he's taken him out."

"How would that work?" Jenny asked, starting the engine. "Say Zorro sprayed Lol, then got you as a target and sprayed you, too? Would he win, even though there are other players left in the game?"

"Doubt it," Green said.

"It's the last person standing, so I suppose he'd be given a new target laminate. Hold on, I need to stop for gas."

They pulled up at the gas station.

"Pick up a bottle of water, too," Green suggested.

When she got back into the car she handed him a can of cola.

"No water left." She handed him a copy of the city newspaper. WATER SUPPLIES LIMITED TO FOUR HOURS A DAY, the headline said.

When they got back to Green's, the coast was clear. Inside, he tried to make coffee. No water came from the tap. The paper didn't lie.

"So much for our showers," Green said. "Does the paper say when the water's coming on?"

"It varies from area to area," Jenny told him. "According to this, we could be rationed to two hours a day by next weekend. That's if it doesn't rain this week."

"Should make the end of the game interesting," Green told her, pouring the last of his bottled water into the electric kettle.

 Second Sunday 1:06 P.M.
HAN

"Hannah! Lunch!" This was Mom's fourth, exasperated yell. Han was laying in bed. She needed to conserve her energy to catch Chris. Later, she would do some homework, to get back in her teachers' good books. Her plan this week was to show up for attendance and dip out only when she had a lead on Chris. She had no idea who her own assassin was, but the likelihood was she'd just had a new one assigned. School was a good place to hide.

"You're late," Mom said when Han finally came down.

"At least I'm here," Han pointed out.

"I don't suppose there's any point in asking what you've been up to all week?"

"Not really."

"These stories about school friends and camp and homework aren't very convincing, you know. I remember what it was like to be your age. I know you're seeing a boy."

"If you already know, you don't need to ask me, do you?"

"You don't deny it, then?"

"I want to see the news," Han said, turning on the TV. She wished she could change the conversation as easily as she could the TV channel.

"Not while we're eating," Mom said, taking the remote from Han. A commercial break ended and the local news began.

"*Organizers may be forced to cancel what is being billed as the world's biggest-ever water fight, scheduled to take place in City Park this coming Saturday. The reason: a water shortage that has reduced most parts of the city to just four hours a day of water. Organizers admit that playing the game might be in 'bad taste' during the current drought but say that, currently, they plan to go ahead with all players using recycled water.*

"*Meanwhile, the water gun assassination game that has seen hijinks all over the city for the last two weeks is due to end this week.*"

Mom glanced at the screen, then piled noodles onto Han's plate. She seemed to have forgotten about turning the TV off.

"Do you remember how you and your brother used to play with water pistols all the time?" she asked Han.

"Sure," Han said awkwardly. She and Mom never discussed Chris, not since he left home.

"*The game has drawn players of all ages and backgrounds, from students to TV personalities.*"

The screen showed a game show host being sprayed by someone out of shot. The celebrity began to plug a TV documentary about his involvement in the game.

"If he were still here, Chris would have joined this game," Mom said. The screen showed players spraying and being sprayed. Their shots didn't look real. There was nothing at stake in them. The players—if they really were players—were hamming it up for the camera.

"*We tried to get an interview with the game's mysterious organizer, who calls himself the gamekeeper, but he insists that he will give no interviews until the contest is over, and won't reveal how many players remain to be eliminated. Who are the favorites? Two of the last three contests have been won by the same player, who calls himself Zorro.*"

The screen cut to images of a thin, long-haired guy at an end-of-game party. He had a pencil mustache and a sly smile. Then the picture cut to an Academy student called Cliff, who described how Zorro had taken him out in the first minute of the game. Han recognized Cliff. He was the guy she'd seen driving Chris around.

"Zorro's a legend in the game, but there's a player called Mac who I think can beat him. He's got the kind of—"

"Eat your noodles!" Mom said. "You're thin enough as it is." She turned off the TV, cutting off Cliff in mid-flow. Mom had made no connection between Han's long, recent absences and the report they'd just been watching. Good. Han stuffed a prawn into her mouth.

"I'm staying over at Erin's tonight," she said, looking at her food rather than her mother. "I'll go to school from there tomorrow."

"If you say so," Mom said. "But be warned, I'm seeing the principal on Tuesday. She asked me to come in. It better not be about your attendance."

WEEK THREE

Third Monday 10:03 A.M.

GREEN

Green was at work. He could have taken the day off, but spring break was over and Jenny had had to go to school, so there was no point. She'd already called him to say that Lol was at school, too. Green was safe. For now.

Lol might try to win Jenny back. There was nothing Green could do to stop him. All he could do was find and spray Zorro. His target could be anywhere in the city. Without Jenny's car, there was no point in Green hanging around near his target's home. Even if Zorro went there, Green was way too conspicuous. So he did what he did whenever he wasn't out on call. He surfed the Net, reading up on Zorro's past exploits, looking for clues on how to catch him.

Zorro wasn't like the other players. He wasn't boastful about his kills. He let his legend be built up by the people he sprayed.

One moment the street was empty. I turned around and he was right behind me.

A high-security building, the highest. But he managed to get a job as a security guard.

The mustache should have been a giveaway, but it was a fancy dress party and he had the figure of a woman. No prizes for guessing where he hid his water balloons . . .

Zorro's mustache was a constant. The long hair was sometimes tied back or hidden under a shirt. He was good at getting people to invite him into their homes, and it seemed he really did work in IT. *He's like my mirror image,* Green thought, *a thin, hairier version of me.* He scanned the most recent postings on the game Web site. There was a blog where active players recounted their exploits. When he clicked on refresh a new entry appeared. The author called himself Senile.

Looks like my days are numbered, Senile wrote. *I spotted Zorro in the complex today, dressed as an orderly. He's not allowed to spray me here but can get me anytime I leave. So I'm stuck inside, with no chance of spraying my target. He'll spray me sooner or later, but I plan to make him wait. Anyone got any advice on how to escape this creep?*

Green sent Senile a private message. It ended, *We might be able to help each other, but once he knows that you know, we're in trouble. Delete your blog entry.* Then he waited. There was a call. He had to visit one of the Academy IT centers, replace a frozen monitor. When he got back, he pressed refresh. Senile's entry about Zorro was gone. Green checked his e-mail. Senile had sent his phone, address, and room number. Green e-mailed the gamekeeper, asking for a rule clarification. Then he texted

Jenny. Lol was still in school. Green was safe to leave. He called a taxi. Finally, he phoned his boss.

"Need to take some personal time. Got to visit this really old guy in a home on the other side of town. He's in trouble."

"A relative?" the head of IT asked.

"Even closer than that," Green said, and hung up.

As he waited for the taxi, Green checked his e-mail and thought about texting Jenny a third time, telling her where he was going. But suppose, now that they were back at school together, Lol had already persuaded Jenny to go out with him again? He might get hold of her messages. Did Green trust Jenny to stay with him? Best, he decided, not to test that. He would call Jenny again only when he needed her. Even better, he would call her when he had eliminated Zorro.

Third Monday 1:13 P.M.
MAC

Mac stood on a busy corner in the business district, watching the street. Last night he'd dreamed of a girl on a bicycle. He'd never dreamed about D.C., but the girl who'd sprayed D.C., she was different. He'd only seen her from behind, yet sensed it at once. She was the one who was going to spray him. She would eliminate him from the game. His new assassin knew where he lived. And she knew where he had been hiding. Mac had nowhere to go.

There he was, Mac's new target. Crossing the road on his lunch hour, not a care in the world. He wore a Beatles mop-top wig—that was, unless his hair had grown a great deal since the photo on the target laminate. It wasn't much of a disguise. In fact, it drew attention to him. The player's name, Badmonkey, suggested he didn't take the game too seriously. In which case, how come he had gotten this far?

Mac relaxed. All he had to do was cross the street, catch up to his target, spray him from behind, take his laminate, and get back in Cliff's car, which was waiting down the street. It was really good of Cliff, Maiko, and Shell to keep helping him. Mac liked Shell. If things were different, he might've gotten something going with her.

The light changed. Mac crossed the street, walking past the busy shops along the dry street. In this part of the city, where serious money was made, everything looked clean, but the air still reeked of sewers and drains. Rats scuttled along the gutters. Badmonkey turned a corner at the end of the block. His office was another two blocks away. Mac had time to catch up and spray him before he reached the exclusion zone, which was within one block of work.

"Hey! Let go!" Arms lifted Mac. They belonged to two guys in their twenties. Both looked like bodybuilders, bodyguards, or both.

"Turn around, pal. Make tracks."

"You work for Badmonkey?"

The men turned Mac so that he was facing in the opposite direction. Then they put him back on the ground. A young woman stood in front of him. She was dressed in classic office garb, a gray flannel skirt and jacket, despite the heat. And she was taking photos of him with a digital camera. One of the thugs spoke.

"None of your business who we work for, pal, but you're not wanted around here. Now get lost. Understood?"

"Understood."

It was already too late for Mac to catch his target. He started walking away from the bodyguards and the photographer. This one was going to be harder than he'd thought.

Third Monday 1:15 P.M.
HAN

After afternoon attendance, Han slipped out of school and caught the train into the city. She had handed in her homework earlier, and made nice with teachers whose lessons she'd missed the week before vacation. There would still be trouble when Mom went to see the principal tomorrow. Han couldn't decide how to play that one. She could be all sweetness and light and lie through her teeth. Or she could go AWOL.

Growing up, Han had idolized her big brother. Dad was always working. Chris was around, looking after her when Mom was busy, playing with her. Some days, he put her before school and his friends. Then Dad left. Chris became remote—more so when Mom met someone new, so quickly, and proceeded to marry him. (Okay, Han wasn't stupid. She eventually worked out that Mom was already seeing husband number two and he was the reason why Dad left.)

Han was only a kid. She cleaved to her new stepdad. Chris, as soon as he turned sixteen, went to live with his father. There was nothing Mom could do. *Your brother will come back in time,* Mom said. Han wasn't convinced, even then. Now, all this time later, he was still gone. So was her dad. He died two and a half years ago. Han didn't find out until after the funeral.

The apartment was as she'd left it. No sign that anyone was watching. Han checked the game's Web site. Reading between the lines, she learned there weren't many players left. Nobody had written about D.C. being sprayed yet. A couple of people were talking about Mac as a potential winner, after he got the Invisible Man, but he only had three kills compared to Han's five. Zorro remained the favorite, with six kills. Badmonkey, who seemed to have come from nowhere, had the same number.

There were no new e-mails from the gamekeeper. No mail of any kind waiting for Han. Good. She hadn't been discovered.

Who was Mac's target? If Han knew that, she would know where to look for him, but the Web site offered no clue. This was an impossible game, Han decided. How could you win it without a team, or at least a bunch of helpers, as Chris had? Funny. Her brother had never been terribly good at making friends. He was a loner, like her. He used to say she was his only friend. And then she wasn't.

Time to get out. Han's assassin would be watching this

place. She called for a taxi, requesting the woman driver who had picked her up before. The driver would know to park directly outside the door, keeping Han covered.

First, Han would go to the station, where, earlier, she had left her bike locked up. Then she would comb the city, paying particular attention to the City Academy campus, searching for Chris.

Third Monday 1:25 P.M.
GREEN

Green stayed outside the complex, watching through an open door. Lunchtime was winding down. No sign of Zorro. Green didn't want to alert the target to his presence. Zorro was bound to recognize him from their encounter on day one. He would know why Green was there. If Green didn't take him by surprise, he'd be gone before Green got close enough to spray him.

The name Senile worried Green a little. Was it a joke or a confession? Green's grandparents were in their mid-sixties. He was used to being around old people. But most of the people in the dining area looked considerably older than his grandparents. Except for the orderlies, who wore green overalls. One of them approached him.

"Looking for someone?"

"Yes. Mr Pappas. Room 207."

"That way."

Green hurried down a well-lit corridor. The pale pink walls were decorated with framed photographs of pets. Were the pictures to substitute for the animals that residents weren't allowed to keep? Despite the heat outside, the building smelled antiseptic, oppressively clean. Green pressed the buzzer on the door of room 207. The door opened automatically onto a crowded room.

"You must be Green." The speaker wore wire-rimmed spectacles with lenses as thick as a finger. Above them were bushy black eyebrows. He looked about seventy, maybe older.

"Pleased to meet you," Green said, reaching out his hand. "What should I call you?"

"I'm Niles." He held out his hand. Green had to lean down to shake it, for the old man was in an electric wheelchair.

"What do you think of my little empire?" Niles asked.

Green looked around. The room was a combination of Green's apartment and his office. There was computer equipment everywhere, with several monitors, at least four hard drives, and some seriously high-quality surveillance equipment. Shoved in the corner of the room, surrounded by books and magazines, was a single bed.

"Awesome!" Green said. "How did you get hold of all this stuff?"

"Mail order, mostly. I assemble it myself."

"I'm impressed that you've managed to stay in the game this long given your . . . um, disability. Is that chair for real?"

"An accident when I was a teenager. But it didn't stop me

having a family or a good career. Or playing this game. In fact, until now, the wheelchair's turned out to be very handy in hunting my targets. Easy to get around. Lots of places to hide weapons. And people tend not to suspect a cripple."

"Must be hard to get away from your assassins, though."

"Not really. I can't be sprayed in the complex. It's only when I leave that I'm in danger. And I only leave when I'm on a job. Also, I have lots of help. Plenty of people here without much else to do."

"Good point," Green said.

"But Zorro is a nuisance. He's been my assassin for five days. He got a job here, perfectly legitimately, so I can't have him thrown out. But he always seems to be around. I want to get out and spray my new target, but each time I've tried to leave, he's been outside. My friends have tried all kinds of distraction techniques. No luck."

"But now you've found his assassin."

"Indeed. How many kills do you have?"

"Three. You?"

"Four. I've had a good run. I never expected to win. But maybe I can help the eventual winner."

Green and Niles exchanged a complicit look. "You mean you'd . . . ?"

"Yes," Niles said. "I'm willing to act as bait."

SHELL

Cliff and Shell had classes that finished at five. They met Maiko afterward and drove over to get Mac. He was waiting in the men's locker room of a local gym. He'd had a shower and his blond hair was mussed, fresh smelling in the dry, dusty heat.

Shell was at the wheel of Cliff's car. According to his firm's Web site, Badmonkey's office closed at 5:30. However, there was no guarantee that he would leave then. The boss could go home whenever he wanted to.

The traffic was heavy. Shell wasn't used to driving in rush hour. When she got to the office block, it was nearly quarter to six. The streets were so busy, it would be easy to miss the target.

"Why are you so sure he leaves by foot?" Cliff asked Mac. "If it was me, and I was the boss, I'd use a chauffeur-driven car."

"Arrogance? He wants to prove he can do his job, walk around like a free man, and make his kills. Hold on, I think that's him!"

A man in a mop-top wig was leaving the office by foot. He melted into the crowd of commuters on the pavement.

"There!" Mac pointed out. "Five paces behind him. Those are his bodyguards."

"And where's the woman you told us about?" Shell asked from the driver's seat.

"I don't see her, but she was small," Mac said. "She's probably nearby."

"Okay," Cliff said. "Let's stick to the plan. Maiko and I take out the bodyguards. Shell stays in the car and distracts the woman, if necessary, but mainly she keeps an eye out for the chick on the bike."

Badmonkey was nearly at the end of the block now. He was waiting for the lights to change. Shell drove past him. There was no need for her to pull over to the curb. That would draw attention to herself. The traffic was backed up, so they were stationary most of the time. That was often the way in the city. At rush hour, a pedestrian could easily outpace a driver.

Cliff and Maiko got out of the car first. Mac, keeping his head down, followed them. *This could all be over in seconds,* Shell thought. She kept checking her rearview mirror. No sign of a bike assassin. On the path beside her, commuters kept coming. She couldn't see Mac or the others among them.

The traffic started up again and the car behind her honked. Shell had to move. Once she got to the next block, the plan was for her to turn onto a side street and wait for them. But the traffic was moving slowly. The spraying might be over before she made it to them. She looked in her rearview mirror again. Nothing. She couldn't see Cliff, Maiko, or Mac. It gave her a bad feeling.

GREEN

The hours dragged. There had been no sign of Zorro all afternoon, but Niles said not to worry. The orderlies' shifts were about to change. Green sat next to Niles in the activities room, playing chess. If anyone asked, Green was Niles's nephew.

"You're not half bad at this game," Niles told Green. "If you ever want a rematch when all this is over, you know where to find me."

"I might just do that," Green said.

"Handsome boy your age, I expect you have several women around, keeping you busy. That's what I was like at eighteen."

"There's just the one," Green said, taking a pawn.

"Tell me about her."

Green told the old man how he'd met Jenny, how he couldn't exactly trust her but wanted to. "Do you think I should invite her over here?" he asked Niles.

"Of course you should. This is only a game, Green. If she betrays you, then at least you know you tried. If she helps you, maybe you have a partner for life. There's nothing more valuable."

An orderly came in, pushing a drinks cart. Green tensed up. His hand rushed to the water pistol in his pocket. It had a short effective range, but there was also a primed Super Soaker beneath the seat of Niles's wheelchair. A water weapon for any circumstance. Was he allowed to use them here? He'd decided to shoot first, ask that question later. Anyway, this wasn't Zorro. This orderly was too old and overweight to be the target in disguise.

"When did you last see your assassin?" Green asked.

"Two days ago. He was helping my next-door neighbor to the bathroom. He winked at me. He knows that I know."

"Still with the mustache and the ponytail?"

"Oh yes."

"Strange that he should let you see him."

"I've been reading up on past tournaments," Niles said. "By this stage of the game, players usually know who their assassin is. It tends to slow things down. But you're right, you discovered who your assassin was when he tried to spray you. Whereas, with Zorro, it's almost like he wants to taunt me. It would give me great pleasure for you to see him off."

Third Monday 5:32 P.M.
SHELL

Two minutes after Shell pulled over, Mac, Cliff, and Maiko were back in the car.

"Did you get him?" Shell asked, though the looks on their faces told her all she needed to know.

"It wasn't Badmonkey," Mac said. "He looked right from a distance, but that was because of the black wig and the

169

bodyguards behind. As soon as I sprayed him, I knew it was wrong. He was a decoy."

"So the real Badmonkey is off attacking his own target?"

"And he's on to our method of attack," Cliff pointed out.

They drove in silence for a while, inching their way through the still heavy traffic.

"I think we should go and check out his home," Maiko said.

"Let's get some dinner first," Cliff suggested.

"I'm not going back to the Academy," Mac said. "Too risky."

"Your assassin's as likely to be at your apartment," Shell said.

"I haven't been there for a week. Maybe I should check in. The assassin probably won't expect me to turn up there. It's not too risky."

"I'm hungry!" Maiko complained.

"I'll drop you two off first," Shell offered, "then take Mac. That's if it's okay for me to use the car, Cliff?"

Cliff nodded. Shell dropped him and Maiko just outside their dorm. No sign of the assassin waiting. Mac gave her directions for the last couple of streets before his apartment. They pulled up to one of the shabbiest parts of town, not far from where Shell had hunted Han, before she was eliminated from the game. She stopped right outside.

"Looks clear," Mac said.

Shell turned to him. "Want me to come in with you?"

"There's no need."

"Suppose your assassin does come by? You'll be trapped in there. And if you haven't been home for a week, you're going to need supplies. I can get them for you."

"It's okay," Mac said. "Really."

"I know what guys are like," Shell said. "Don't worry. However messy it is, the place can't be worse than what I'm imagining."

"It's not that," Mac said.

"Give me the keys," Shell said. "I can make sure it's clear before you get out."

"Okay." Mac looked embarrassed as he handed Shell the keys. She looked up and down the street. Nobody around. She opened the outer door and walked up to Mac's first-floor apartment. Again, it was quiet. She could have gone back for Mac at once, but something made her unlock the door first. She wanted to see what it was like without Mac there to monitor her reaction.

Shell wasn't sure what kind of mangy flea pit she expected to see, but it was nothing like what she found. Mac, she realized at once, had been lying to her. He had been lying to them all.

Third Monday 5:45 P.M.
GREEN

"Checkmate in three," Niles said, then showed Green the combination of moves that meant he was bound to lose. "Is that your girlfriend?"

Jenny walked across the room, looking prettier than ever. She appeared to be alone.

"What are you doing out in the open?" she asked Green. "Won't Zorro recognize you?"

"Doesn't matter if he does, long as I get to him first."

"Too risky," she said.

"We do have a plan," Niles told her. "Your friend here was waiting for you to arrive."

"What's the word on Lol?" Green asked. "Did he follow you?"

"As if he'd tell me. But I overheard him talking to some of his friends. I think they're going to wait for you at the Academy."

"Great. So I won't be able to go home tonight."

"True. But Lol doesn't know I'm seeing you, so you should be safe with me. I spoke with my mom before I borrowed her car. She says you can stay in our spare room for the last few days of the game. Is that okay?"

"Okay? That's awesome!"

"Good. Look, I had to explain who you were, but I was too embarrassed to go into how I tried to trick you for Lol—it makes me sound like such a bitch and I'm not, not really."

"Of course you're not," Green said. "What did you tell her?"

"I told her that you were my new boyfriend. I hope that's okay."

"Fine," Green said, hoping that his face hadn't gone red. "Have a seat. Niles is going to explain our plan."

SHELL

Mac's apartment looked shabby and squalid from the outside. Inside, it was a palace, filled with pricey toys. It had shiny floorboards, an expensive stereo, handmade blinds, and a state-of-the-art kitchen area. It must cost a fortune to rent, or an unimaginable amount to own. Shell looked at the leather sofa, the framed paintings on the wall. The TV alone would have cost all of her spending money for the year. How could such a young guy afford a place like this?

There were footsteps on the stairwell. She spun around. Mac had followed her in.

"I got fed up of waiting," he said. "Street was clear."

"You've got some explaining to do," Shell told Mac. "How come somebody who works in a burger bar lives in a place like this?"

"Right question," Mac said. "Wrong way around. The question you should have asked was: How come someone like me was working in a burger bar? I got the job because, to enter the game, you had to live and work in the area where the game was played. So I rented this place and found a job."

"Why aren't you in school, or something?"

"I'm rich."

"How come? You're from a rich family?"

"Yes. I'm the only son. Dad's dead. I inherited everything."

"Nice," Shell said. But it wasn't nice, not at all. Shell only respected people who had to work for what they had.

"So Maiko, Cliff, and me have been taking time out of our lives to help a poor little rich boy who can afford to buy anything he wants."

"I can't pay people to help me," Mac told her. "If I'm going to win, I have to win fair and square; otherwise, it's meaningless. You guys helped me because you like me, and because you got thrown out of the game early on, and you missed the thrill. Isn't that true?"

Shell didn't know how to reply. She'd helped Mac because she had a crush on him. As for the others, it was usually harder to understand other people's motivations than it was to be honest about your own. Maybe Cliff was in it for the thrill. But to begin with, he had stayed involved because he was making a move on Shell. When that failed, he had settled for Maiko. Now Shell was stuck with Mac the Millionaire, who was merely using her to stay in the game. He wasn't interested in her as a friend, certainly not as a girlfriend. In a few days, win or lose, he'd be gone.

"To be honest," she said, "I don't know what I was thinking. But now I know what you are, you don't need my help anymore. I'm out of here."

"Wait!" Mac said. "This has come out all wrong. I really like you, Shell. I thought you'd be pleased when you found out I wasn't just a bum. . . ."

"Being rich doesn't stop you from being a bum."

"You know, if I lived around here, you're the sort of girl I'd want to be with. When you kissed me I wanted to . . . you know. But it wouldn't be fair, when I knew I'd be gone as soon as I was out of the game. I've only got three kills. I could have been out at any moment."

"You can't be that interested if you'd be gone as soon as you're out of the game," Shell said.

"I still like you," Mac told her. "And I still need your help. Please."

"I'll think about it," Shell said. "I'll call you when I've made up my mind. In the meantime, good luck with Badmonkey. I reckon you two were made for each other."

She turned and hurried out of the open door and down the stairs, before Mac could see that she was crying. On the dusty street outside, she noticed a girl on a bike. Good luck to her.

Third Monday 7:22 P.M.
GREEN

The evening meal in Senile's complex had been over for twenty minutes. There was still no sign of Zorro.

"Maybe he made us earlier," Green said.

"Made?" Niles said. "What is this, a mafia movie?"

"I could try to sneak into the office," Jenny suggested, "see if he's scheduled to work tonight."

"Whether he's working or not," Niles told them, "he'll want a kill. Look!"

His computer screen was open to the game's Web site. It showed a new leader, claiming a total of seven kills: a player who called himself Badmonkey.

Nobody knows what Badmonkey looks like, someone called Peg had written. *All I saw of him was a cheap wig, probably plastic, that made him look like a member of a historical singing group. He had the most powerful water weapon I have ever come across. I was at the far side of the cinema. I thought I was safe, surrounded by friends. Yet, in the moment that the lights went down, my spraying days ended. At least I lost to a worthy adversary. I congratulate you, Badmonkey!*

"Badmonkey?" Jenny said. "What kind of a stupid name is that?"

"Never mind," Niles said. "Jenny, I want you to call me a taxi, one of the big limousine type ones with a special lift for wheelchairs."

"Where are you going?" Jenny asked.

"Nowhere."

 Third Monday 7:49 P.M.
HAN

Han's target was home. During the two weeks Han had been squatting in the apartment, her brother had only been two streets away. Why, with all his money, did he choose to live somewhere so ghetto? Han hid in a doorway that was within spraying range of Chris's doorway but not visible from his upstairs window. She'd seen his girlfriend leave two hours before. There had been no movement since. She had him cornered at last.

Tomorrow was the meeting with the principal. Han was supposed to be home tonight. What if she called Mom and explained herself? How would Mom react? Chris had hurt her just as much as he had hurt Han. But if Han got caught, Mom would lose her, too. She'd probably tell Han to leave well enough alone.

A dog barked. Impatient, Han primed her Super Soaker again. She wanted the maximum possible range. The apartment had no rear entrance. Nor was there a window at the back that Chris could jump out of. There was no fire escape at the back—she'd checked—so escaping that way wasn't an option. He would have to . . .

Why hadn't she thought of that before? The city had been on a high fire alert for weeks now. It hadn't rained once during the course of the game. With the heat wave and the water shortage house fires spread quickly. And nobody would risk their life for a stupid game, no matter how dedicated they were to winning it.

There was a warehouse downtown that sold the kind of thing she needed. Han hoped that it stayed open late.

GREEN

Many of the complex's residents had already gone to bed. Green waited in the empty kitchen. His target wouldn't be expecting an attack from here. Zorro might be under the impression that the whole complex counted as his workplace, so he was safe. Green had been concerned by this. That was why he'd e-mailed the gamekeeper. If somebody got a new job during the course of the game, he'd asked, was their new workplace an exclusion zone? He'd gotten an immediate reply. No. So, if Green saw Zorro, he could spray him.

Green felt his phone vibrate. A text from Jenny. The taxi's arriving. Time to get into position. He pushed open the kitchen's emergency exit and looked around. All clear. He was in the shadowy loading area. Zorro wouldn't wait here. From this side of the complex, you could see the entrance, where Senile's taxi was waiting, but it was impossible to get a shot at it. There were two places where Zorro might shoot from. A narrow upstairs window. That was locked when Green tried it earlier, but the assassin might have a key. More likely, he would shoot from the smoking area, to the right of the entrance. There were always one or two people hanging out there. It was within range of the area where taxis waited. And it was within range of where Green was standing now. Just.

Niles had to make his way to the taxi alone. If Jenny

escorted him, Zorro might suspect that she was his assassin and use avoidance tactics. They wanted Zorro to think that Senile thought he wasn't around, so it was safe to go outside. Trouble was, Zorro might really be away. Otherwise, where had he been hiding all evening?

The doors to the main entrance opened. The taxi driver already had his ramp down. If this was to look convincing, Niles had to move into the taxi quickly. Green watched everything on the round circular mirror that was mounted on the wall beside him. The mirror was there so that delivery vans exiting the loading bay didn't scrape a car on their way out. The view wasn't perfect but it was good enough. In a few paces, Green could step out into full view of the entrance. He gave his Super Soaker two more pumps, to maximize the pressure.

Green's plan was to spray Zorro just as he was taking the target laminate from Niles. But when he turned the corner, things weren't going according to the plan. The wheelchair was already on the ramp. Once Niles was sealed inside the car, he was safe. Where was the assassin? Did Zorro suspect a trap? If so, he might wait for his target to return. But that didn't add up. What if Senile didn't return? What if he was escaping somewhere else and this would be Zorro's last chance to spray him? No, Zorro couldn't take that chance. So why hadn't he come out?

If Green were Zorro, what would he do? In the taxi's mirror, Green saw Niles give an anxious glance in his direction. He hadn't been sprayed. His sacrifice had been pointless. Unless ... suddenly, Green worked out what he would do in Zorro's situation. He only had a few seconds. The wheelchair was about to lock into place. Once that happened, the taxi door would automatically close and . . . Green ran out of the parking bay, into the entrance area, not caring who saw him.

"Stop!" he shouted to Niles. "Don't let him close the door!"

Too late. The door slid automatically across. Niles gave Green a bewildered stare. The taxi didn't move, though. The driver smiled at Green, then turned to his sole passenger, a compact water pistol in his hand. Senile's sacrifice was for nothing. Zorro soaked him, then took his laminate.

Green watched as Zorro closed the glass partition between driver and passenger, then unloaded the wheelchair. The damp, disabled man steered himself back into the complex. Zorro gave Green a regal wave as he drove off. Now he knew who his assassin was. Green's small advantage was gone.

"He outsmarted us," Niles told Green in his most philo-sophical voice. "Ah well, you knew he was good."

"It was worth a try," Jenny said. She gave Niles a hug, then turned to Green. "Come on, I'll drive you home."

"Wait," Green said. "Niles, do you mind telling me who your next target was? It's my best way of getting to Zorro."

"It's a tough one," Niles said. "A young girl. She's never where she's supposed to be and I only caught a fleeting glimpse of her once, riding a bike. She calls herself Han."

MAC

Mac was tempted to book a hotel room for the night. It would be safer than going home, or staying with Shell and Cliff, even presuming they'd forgiven him for misleading them. He didn't lie. He had never claimed to be poor. People assumed Mac was broke because he worked in a burger bar. So he acted broke. Slumming it was part of the experience of the game. That was why he was reluctant to stay in a hotel tonight, even though he could easily afford one.

He didn't feel like going back to his apartment, though. Shell had soured it for him. And there might be an assassin waiting outside.

You could take slumming it too far. Living in a rough part of town was one thing, but Mac needed a comfortable apartment for the rare occasions that he was there—after all, he might be trapped inside it for ages. The place he was renting was so decked out, Mac reckoned it belonged to a criminal of some kind. It had a state-of-the-art entertainment center, high-speed Internet, and central air to keep out the torrid summer heat.

Mac had only spent a couple of nights in his place since the game began. He had slept on Ben's floor and the floor of Cliff's room. Any discomfort was well worth it for the advantage it gave him in the game. He'd made it to the final week of the game on his third attempt. Now he had his toughest target yet.

Badmonkey must have been out tonight, for Mac had waited by his smart apartment all evening, carefully concealed between two parked cars.

Maybe he should buy himself a car for the last week of the game. Mac didn't have a license in this country, or, indeed, in any country, but he could drive. At this stage, however, it was probably cheaper and easier to use taxis, as he was doing now.

"Which house is it?"

"Just go around the corner."

Another reason Mac suspected that his apartment's owner was crooked was that it had a useful, secret escape route. You'd never have guessed, but the building had a fire door on the second floor. This led to a narrow passageway linking four houses on the street, with an exit in the corner house, which had an old-fashioned iron fire escape. Mac didn't want to use it often as a way in, or out. If he did, it wouldn't stay secret for long. But it certainly came in handy at times when he was likely to be watched, like now.

"Sorry," the driver said. "Can't get down this road. Looks like there's something going on."

Mac swore. "Just go around the other way, would you?"

"Don't think I can. It's the fire department, see? They're connected to the water main. They're blocking the next street, too."

"Can you get a bit closer?" Mac didn't want to get out of the car, but he was getting an uncomfortable feeling.

"Too dangerous. See that smoke? I think it's a fire."

"Wait here. I'll be right back."

"Fare first, please."

"I'm leaving my bag," Mac said. "I'll be right back."

"No offense, but I've had people pull tricks on me before. You know how it is, they leave a bag full of garbage and . . ."

Mac handed him a large bill. "I'll be back. Wait here."

He hurried around the corner. There were two fire engines on his street. He turned to one of the firefighters.

"Was anybody hurt?"

"Hardly. There was no fire. Some joker set off three smoke bombs in the entrance hall. We covered it in foam before we realized there was no danger. Live there?"

"Yeah. First floor."

"Most people have gone back to their apartments now, but there'll be a bit of a smell. And you're probably better off going in the back way. The entrance hall's a real mess."

Third Tuesday 10:27 A.M.
GREEN

Jenny's home was just inside the city limits but felt like it belonged to a different world. Inside, the house was airy and comfortable. It had running water, so Green was able to take a shower when he got up. Jenny didn't have a class until 11:15, so she shared a late breakfast with Green. Her mother cooked eggs, acting as chaperone. She kept asking Green questions: Why wasn't he in school? How many serious girlfriends had he had before? Green ducked them as best he could. He was taking a year off and didn't need to go to college, though he probably would. With his IT skills, he could get a job anywhere. He could follow Jenny anywhere, if she was seriously interested in him—but he didn't say this out loud.

The texts started to flood in at 10:30, which was morning break. At first, Jenny ignored them, busy eating her eggs. Then she got one that drew her attention.

"It's Lol," she said. "I'd better see what he wants. If he finds out you're staying here, we could be in trouble." She opened the text. "Oh my . . ." Her eyes widened and she passed the phone to Green.

"What is it?" her mom said.

"Lol got sprayed last night. He wants to know if his assassin has sprayed Green already. Evidently he's really good."

Green passed the phone back. Jenny went through her other messages. "I don't believe this!" she told him. "Now there are only five players left. You've made it to the last five! That's incredible."

"It's not bad," Green said, "but I have to spray Zorro and avoid being sprayed by . . . can we check the game Web site? I should be able to work out who my assassin is."

"We've got five minutes," Jenny said. "I'll just boot up my laptop."

"Or you could look out the window," Jenny's mom told them. "There's a man in a three-piece suit and a Beatles wig getting out of a limousine. Do you think by any chance that could be him?"

SHELL

"Don't think that because I let you sleep on my floor last night, we're a team again," Shell told Mac. "If someone hadn't set fire to your place..."

"It was only a smoke bomb, the firefighters said."

"Did you report it to the gamekeeper yet?"

"I e-mailed him while you were making breakfast. I'm not sure whether my assassin was breaking the rules or not. But the firefighters and the other residents weren't too happy."

"Personally, I think it was a clever move. If you'd been in, your assassin would have smoked you out. Too bad they failed."

Shell knew she'd gone too far but didn't care. Mac took a deep breath before replying.

"Listen, Shell. I never meant to lie to you. I was careful not to get involved ... romantically, or whatever you want to call it. I'm only in the city to play the game."

"As you've made very clear. So go on. Clear out. Play."

"I still need your help."

"Why should I give it?"

"Because we're friends? Look, most girls I've met are pretty happy that I'm rich."

"I'm not most girls," Shell said. "And why should I be impressed by you, just because you've inherited money? And even if I was interested ... romantically, which I'm not, you're going to be somewhere else next week. You're not exactly a sure thing."

"I . . . I don't know where I'll be, either," Mac said. "I'm an orphan. Since my dad died, I don't need to work. I've got nothing going on except this game. And, right now, you're the closest friend I've got."

Despite her anger, Shell felt sorry for him. If she was honest with herself, he hadn't encouraged her, except as a friend. Nor had he lied to her, not exactly. She was angry because he had hidden part of his life from her. But maybe that was his right.

Shell chose her next words carefully.

"Okay. I'll help you to try and find Badmonkey. I've come this far, I'd like to see how the game ends. Have you looked at the Web site this morning? According to the betting, he and Zorro are joint favorites."

"Really?"

"Really. That means there are only five players left. And you're one of them."

 Third Tuesday 10:38 A.M.
GREEN

Jenny's mom drove her to school, leaving Green behind. He was trapped in his girlfriend's house. If she *was* his girlfriend. Green could have gone with Jenny but didn't want his assassin to know that he was here. He should have known that Lol would out him to whoever his new assassin was. The guy outside was either Mac or Badmonkey. Either would be very dangerous. The Beatles wig suggested that it was Badmonkey, but the assassin could be playing a double bluff.

How far away was Jenny's school? Green needed to get after Zorro but he didn't have a clue where to find him. A car pulled up outside.

"He's still there," Jenny's mom told Green, "lingering behind the driveway. Does he think you're stupid enough to come out?"

"I was rather hoping you'd drive me somewhere," Green said.

"He'd spray you before you got in the car, I'm afraid. I think we can find a way to get rid of him. I could call the police, for instance. Or is that outside the rules of the game?"

"I don't think the police would be too happy. They'd say he's here because I chose to play the game. Sorry. Also, I could do without running into them again because . . ." He explained about the ruse he'd pulled at the central police station.

"That was before you met Jenny, wasn't it? How exactly did you meet Jenny? I know she tried to register for the game but didn't get in."

"Um . . ." Green didn't want to lie, but he didn't want to betray Jenny, either, by letting on how she'd been doing Lol's dirty work. He decided to be circumspect. "We bumped into each other on a bus and got to talking."

Outside, Badmonkey lay in wait, not even bothering to hide.

Third Tuesday 9:44 A.M.
ZED

"At least I got taken out by the top player," Zed said.

She was looking over Yogi's shoulder as he read the game Web site. The odds listed were based on each player's kill results and bets being taken. Badmonkey and Zorro were joint favorites. Next came Mac, then Green, then, finally, Han. There were no other players left in the game.

"It seems so long ago that we were both in it," Yogi said. "We were willing to hide out in that container for three weeks. Can you imagine if we were still there?"

"I can't see us still being a couple if we were," Zed said. "That place was seriously claustrophobic."

The doorbell rang.

"Expecting someone?" Zed asked.

"An informant."

"Here? At our home?"

"Believe me, this is an informant you'll want to meet."

Zed opened the door to a good-looking guy about her own age. His hair was short and he had a small cleft in his chin, which she'd read somewhere denoted selfishness. He gave her a thin smile and said hello in an accent that she couldn't place.

"You look familiar," she said. "Have we met before?"

"Yes, but I was wearing a trench coat and silly glasses."

"Wow!" she said. "You're the gamekeeper."

188

"I am. Is Yogi here?"

"Come in, come in."

Zed got the gamekeeper some water while he introduced himself to Yogi.

"Have you any way of proving that you're you?" her boyfriend asked. "I mean, I met one of your assistants and assumed he was you."

"It doesn't really matter who I am," the gamekeeper said. "This game's been going on for years. I'm not the first gamekeeper and I won't be the last. All of us like to keep our identities secret, to avoid legal difficulties and press interest. So far, over the many years that the game has been played, there have been no serious problems. A few minor injuries, that's all."

"So far?"

"I've come to see you because your entry details show that you're a police officer. Is that correct?"

"It is. You want to see me in an official capacity?"

"I thought it best to come to an officer who I know is friendly to the game. Of course, I understand that you will have to pass on the information I give you. But first, I hope to get your advice."

"Shoot," Yogi said.

"One of our leading players e-mailed me in the early hours this morning. He thinks his home was smokebombed in an attempt to drive him outside where his assassin could spray him."

"Ouch," said Zed. "Was anybody hurt?"

"Luckily not. And the target wasn't home. I may be

overreacting, but I have tried to contact the assassin concerned, who calls herself Han. Unfortunately, all of her details are fake."

"Don't you check people out before they start the game?"

"We meet them all in person. My assistant was a little concerned that she might be underage, which would disqualify her from winning but is hardly a matter of great concern."

"Do you have a photo?"

The gamekeeper handed Yogi a target laminate. "It's not very good. There's too much hair. You can barely make out her face."

"Have you contacted her?"

"I e-mailed her early this morning and asked her to meet me or be eliminated from the game. So far, there's been no response."

"And which player did she try to firebomb?"

"The one who calls himself Mac."

"He's the guy who sprayed me."

"He's a strong player. It appears she thought he was home, but he had a secret exit from the apartment where he was staying and had left before she started the fire."

"How bad was it?"

"I don't know yet. I was hoping that you could find out."

Yogi thought for a moment. "I need to take this to my boss. I'm not on shift until this afternoon. Do you know who's in charge of the arson investigation?"

"Afraid not."

"Any means of getting in touch with this Mac character?"

"I can give you his cell phone number. He doesn't have an address, for obvious reasons."

"Okay. I'll need that, along with your full name and address. This isn't just a game anymore."

The gamekeeper winced when Yogi came out with that cliché, but gave him the information he needed. Then he programmed Yogi's number into his cell and promised to phone if the girl who called herself Han got in touch.

"It might be best if the game finished very quickly, before anybody gets seriously hurt," Yogi told him.

"Point taken," the gamekeeper said. "But I might be overreacting. The fire could have been a coincidence. There have been a lot of fires in the city lately."

Third Tuesday 2:11 P.M.
HAN

Han knew she'd screwed up as soon as the fire alarm went off and she saw people running from the other end of the street. Her brother was always cunning. How was she supposed to know that his apartment had a fire escape three doors away? She'd never been inside. She'd cycled straight over to the fire escape, but everyone was already out. Either Chris escaped then or, more likely, he'd snuck out much earlier and was stalking his victim while she waited to spray him.

The smoke bombs caused more panic than she'd meant to happen. Some damage, too. It had seemed like a good idea at the time. Now she felt bad about smoking everybody out.

Luckily, nobody got hurt when they hurried from their homes. But it had been a stupid, risky thing to do. At least nobody knew who she was. Even if Han had been caught by cameras, she was wearing a bike helmet and face mask.

Right now, she had a more pressing problem to deal with. A buzzer sounded and she stood up.

"You can come in," the principal said, holding her office door open. "Your mother and I have finished talking."

Framed photos of school alumni covered the pale pink walls. Han sat down in an uncomfortable black leather chair with a stiff back. The principal was younger than her mother, and fiercer.

"I know you've had a difficult three years," the principal said. "The divorce, your mother's remarriage, then your father's death, and your brother's disappearance. But you are reaching a crucial point in your school career. Your exam courses are about to start. Mistakes you make now could haunt you for the rest of your life. Skipping school is never wise. And there is no excuse for dishonesty. None at all."

Han put on a serious face. "It's not as bad as you think," she said. "I haven't been with a boy, or on drugs, or anything like that."

"Then where have you been?" Mom asked.

"Do you remember how Chris used to chase me around with a water pistol when we were kids?"

"Yes," Mom said. The Head looked bemused.

"And how he kept a scrapbook about the water war game that travels from city to city?"

"I've read about that," the principal said. "It was a craze at school for a while."

"The thing is, the game's been going on in the city, here, for the last two and a half weeks. So I had to play. That's where I've been, hiding in the city, sneaking up on people with a water pistol. I made it into the final week. But I've been eliminated now. It's all over. I'm sorry about the deception, really. But I'm done. I won't do anything like this again. I'm sorry."

"Well," the principal said. "That is a relief. I do think that this is the sort of matter that ought to be dealt with in the home, rather than at school. So I suggest that you get back to your studies, make up for the work missed, and we'll say no more about it."

"That's very generous of you," Mom said. "Thank you so much for your time."

They left the office. Han was about to head toward the last class of the day when Mom grabbed her by the shoulder.

"Have you seen him?" she asked. "Did you see your brother?"

Third Tuesday 4:14 P.M.

GREEN

Jenny got home from school to find Green reading a newspaper. Her mom had left for work, taking the car with her. Green risked kissing Jenny on the cheek. He was supposed to be her boyfriend, after all.

"Any sign of my assassin?" he asked.

"I think he's gone," Jenny said. "But best not to risk it."

"I have work later tonight."

"I'll borrow Mom's car when she gets back from work and take you there if you want."

"If you could get my shift schedule, I'll bet Badmonkey can, too."

"Don't forget, he's being hunted. He'll have to be careful."

"You're right," Green said. "I've been combing the Web site and message boards, trying to work out who's hunting who. There are five players left and, assuming nobody's been reassigned, Zorro can't be Badmonkey's assassin, so it must be Han or Mac. Trouble is, they're the two players I haven't come across yet. So I wouldn't recognize either of them."

"Is there a way for you to contact one of them and tell them where Badmonkey is?"

"Maybe. But as soon as they've sprayed Badmonkey they could spray me."

Jenny thought for a minute. "You could wait to tell them until there are just three players left, then give up Badmonkey and spray his assassin before he or she has time to take the laminate."

"You've got just the kind of devious mind that I like," Green said.

"I'll take that as a major compliment," Jenny said, and kissed him lightly on the lips.

MAC

Stalemate. Mac had spent all night outside Badmonkey's house, but the businessman had not come home. There was no sign of him near the office, either. He got a taxi back to Shell's, where he checked the game Web site. One more player was down. That left him, his assassin, his target, a guy called Green, and the favorite, Zorro.

His phone vibrated against his chest. Mac didn't recognize the number. Could this be his assassin, taunting him? No, it was the gamekeeper, who Mac had contacted the day before. He had news.

"The girl who calls herself Han hasn't responded to my e-mails, which suggests that she did set off the smoke bombs in your building. I have, reluctantly at this late stage, eliminated her from the game."

"For a few smoke bombs? I thought they were a smart move."

"No. The e-mail I sent told her that two of her victims have complained that she is underage."

Mac was curious about Han. He kept trying to work out what she looked like beneath her face mask. She didn't look that young to him. There was something about her, something familiar. He'd half hoped she would be his final opponent. The smoke bomb was a smart move. If he'd been in, there was a strong chance she would have got him.

195

"She didn't look underage to me."

"Nevertheless, she failed to furnish proof that she's fifteen."

"Does that mean that you've reinstated her last target, D.C.?"

"Wouldn't work. If we did that, I'd have to reinstate all of Han's victims back to the start of the game. My only choice was to make her assassin your assassin. I'm about to inform him of the change."

"Him?"

"All four of the players left in the game are male. You can probably work out which one is your new assassin."

Mac thought for a moment. It couldn't be Badmonkey. That left a guy called Green or . . .

"I'm being pursued by Zorro?"

"I thought it fair to warn you. Good luck."

 Third Wednesday 4:52 P.M.
HAN

School was a shock to the system. Han had no time to sneak off and check the status of the game. At home, she booted up her laptop. Before bringing it back from the squat, she had deleted the e-mail account she'd used for the Spray game. There was a strong risk that Mom would sneak into it and find out that she was still playing. There was also a risk that Han would be disciplined by the gamekeeper for playing dirty. But if he couldn't contact her, he couldn't discipline her, could he?

She checked the game Web site. It was run by fans, not the gamekeeper, but was usually accurate. Things had gone quiet. No kills reported in more than forty-eight hours. Looked like the other four players were being cagey, as well they might. Each was so close to victory. The gamekeeper would have to speed things up if they were going to finish by Sunday. In previous games, he had made himself a target. It would be good if he did so again. She needed a situation that brought Chris out into the open.

Third Wednesday 10:38 P.M.

SHELL

Shell took a taxi to Mac's hotel. She wasn't sure why she was going. Earlier, she'd offered to let him sleep on her floor for another night, but he was worried about Zorro tracking him down there, and refused. Probably for the best. She'd get written up if she was caught with a boy in her room. One time was risky enough, but a repeat was asking for trouble.

Half an hour ago, Mac had called and, against her better judgment, Shell had agreed to visit his temporary home, a plush hotel on the edge of the business district.

"Thanks for coming over," Mac told Shell.

She joined him in a quiet corner of the bar.

"Nice hotel," she said. "Still, I guess you can afford it."

"Hotels are boring. I'd rather be out hunting Badmonkey, but his home security's superb. My only chance of getting him is if I catch him trying to spray Green, and I can't track Green down."

"You should have asked," Shell said. "I know that he works at the City Academy. IT support. We can find him tomorrow. But what if your assassin tracks you here?"

"I used my real name to register, so he'd find it tricky unless he gets a look at me. There are so many hotels in the city, Zorro can't scope them all. But if anyone can get me, he can."

"You were always going to come up against him if you're going to win," Shell pointed out.

"It won't be the first time," Mac told her.

"No?"

"He eliminated me in London, when I played there. First week. I'd just made my first kill and was really proud of myself. I was running for a bus when, suddenly, this guy with a mustache leans out of a passing taxicab and sprays me. Classic move."

"So you've played the game before? In different cities?"

"I didn't break any rules. I got a job in the city working as a porter. In San Francisco, I was a waiter."

"You've been to San Francisco? What's that like?"

"I made it to the second week. It's a fantastic city. You have to go sometime. . . ."

He talked about his travels for an hour. Shell was fascinated, but after a while she noted that he never once asked about her. Nor did he notice when she stopped asking questions or even nodding. Mac had quite an ego on him when he let his hair down. Only when he went to order another drink did he realize that the bar had closed.

"Want to continue the conversation in my suite?"

"I don't think that's a good idea," she said. Mac might be rich and good looking but it had emerged over the evening that he was a year younger than she was. His lack of maturity was beginning to show. She was no longer tempted.

"You're right," he replied. "I need to be sharp tomorrow."

"Could you ask the doorman to call the car around?"

GREEN

Green was planning his endgame. An e-mail from the game-keeper informed him that one player, Han, had been eliminated, for reasons that weren't clear. This meant Green was after Zorro who was after Mac who was after Badmonkey who was after him.

Green was at work. Might as well earn some money while the game was so dead. If this stalemate lasted much longer, he knew, the gamekeeper would initiate some kind of sudden-death shoot-out.

Being big, Green didn't move as fast as some of the other competitors. He was better suited to a tactical game than a physical one. Luckily, he had Jenny to help him. Today she was cutting school, trying to track Badmonkey down. There was no point in her trying to locate the elusive Zorro. The only sensible move was to try and draw the two-time champion to him.

Where Badmonkey was, Mac was likely to be. And where Mac was, Zorro wouldn't be far behind.

Jenny had promised to call at noon and she did, on the dot.

"I found Badmonkey. He's in a chauffeur-driven car that's holed up in the principal's parking space. Can you believe it?"

"Any sign of Mac?"

"No. But I noticed a tall blonde keeping an eye on the car and talking on the phone."

Green knew the girl she meant, a former player named Shell. "Mac could be on his way. Question is, how do we alert Zorro?"

"If he's as good as you say he is, Zorro's onto it already."

Third Thursday 12:02 P.M.

MAC

Mac sat in the back of Cliff's car, hunched up so he couldn't be seen.

"You say this Green guy definitely works around the Academy campus?"

"S'right," Cliff said, and selected the photo he'd taken on his phone. "He showed us his ID card when he came to Shell's room the day before the game began. That's when I took this."

"The card could have been a fake."

"I've seen him around. He works here. So Badmonkey will be watching him here. If Shell's right, Mr. Arrogant is parked in front of the principal's office, just down the road from his IT office."

"He can't spray Green within a block of his work," Mac reminded him.

"Green has to walk farther than a block to get his bus home. Maybe he's got a friend who'll drive him to his apartment, but there are bound to be risky moments, like when he gets out of the car. We have to hope that Green draws Badmonkey out for us."

"Zorro's bound to work out that this is where all the action is."

"You should be safe if you stay in the back of the car most of the time. Nobody can spray you there."

"But I can't spray anybody, either," Mac reflected. "Once I open the window to spray Badmonkey, I'm vulnerable."

Mac's phone rang again. Shell.

"Green's on the move."

Third Thursday 12:06 P.M.
GREEN

Green had his Super Soaker tucked in the huge right pocket of his baggy pants. He kept a tiny water pistol in his left, a red plastic thing he'd got free with a kids' comic: It had surprisingly good range. He should be safe until he got near the bus stop. Jenny would pick him up before that. Where was Badmonkey? Where was Mac? His phone rang.

"Badmonkey's on the move," Jenny said. "I'm following."

"Any sign of the others?"

"Not yet. But I saw the girl getting into an old car."

"We need to open this up," Green told her. "Get everyone out of their cars."

"Then you have to walk somewhere they can't go in a car."

"I'll tell you what," Green said. "Instead of turning right, toward the bus stop, I'll cross the road and head into the library."

"That's not your workplace. You could get sprayed."

"Don't worry. I've spent a lot of time in that library. I know my way around. As long as I get there safely. Where's Badmonkey now?"

"He's a couple of minutes behind you."

"Okay. Pick me up. Give me a lift to the library."

Green stood by the road and waited for her. He imagined a big finale scene in the library, players stalking each other between the aisles. He could picture a Mexican standoff, with all four assassins standing in a circle, each pointing their weapon at their target but reluctant to shoot. If they all shot at once, there could be no winner.

The whole thing was in danger of turning rather juvenile. A librarian was bound to come along and interrupt the scene, throw them out. At which point, they would start spraying, soaking the librarian, each other, and a whole lot of books. The sharpest player—Green, hopefully—would duck behind the book stacks, keep dry, then step out to spray the already soaked other players, and win the game.

Jenny was driving down Academy Road. Ahead of her, a long, gray limo loomed into view. If Badmonkey got out and sprayed him, Green would have a right to complain. He was only a short distance from his workplace, but people had been sprayed just outside campus buildings and the hit had been upheld by the gamekeeper. This wasn't a game you played with a calculator and a measuring tape. Thanks to turning the wrong way, he could be about to be sprayed.

He saw Jenny's car edge right up to the limo. The road was wide but not that wide. Had Badmonkey's driver seen him? Yes, he was accelerating, fast. Green looked for cover, but there was none. His assassin was bound to be quicker than he was. Running away was no good. The library plan had been a bad idea. He should have gone to the bus stop, which was closer.

Just behind Green, the limo screeched to a halt. Another car nearly rear-ended it, stopping just as abruptly. The next moment, Jenny's car skidded around the limo, narrowly missing a bus that was coming in the opposite direction. She opened her passenger door. Green hurried toward her, aware that his assassin was getting out of the limo. At any moment, he would likely feel water on his back. The game would be over.

Jenny's mom's car was a compact. Green had to squeeze in. He struggled to pull the door shut before he was even in the seat.

"Is he behind me?" he asked Jenny.

"Oh, he's behind you, all right," Jenny said. "But you've no need to worry. Turn around."

Green twisted his head back. A middle-aged man with close-cropped hair was on the grass verge. Instead of a water pistol, the man was holding a black, mop-top wig that was sopping wet. Badmonkey was out of the game. Behind Badmonkey was a handsome guy with blond, curly hair. For a moment, Green thought that he was the gamekeeper, come to announce the conclusion of the competition. But then he saw Badmonkey hand over his laminate. The young guy was his new assassin. Mac.

Jenny's car was too small for Green to pump up the pressure on his Super Soaker. He reached into his left pocket for the tiny red water pistol and scanned the horizon.

"Any sign of Zorro?" he asked Jenny.

"No. Doesn't mean he isn't about to make a move. Hold on."

She did a U-turn in the middle of the road, swinging back past the limo and the car that Mac had come in. A student who Green recognized was in the driver's seat. He was the one who'd taken a photo of him with his phone, the day before the game started. There was no sign of Zorro.

"I think we'd better get out of here," Green told Jenny.

 Final Friday 5:00 P.M.
HAN

"Do you really think your brother's in the city for the water fight game?" Mom asked when she got in from school.

"He might be. I thought I'd go along tomorrow, take a look."

"Wouldn't he have contacted us?"

"I'd like to think so," Han said, but she knew how betrayed

Chris had felt when she took sides. She was only ten when he left home. Chris was sixteen. Her brother would be twenty now. Was he still holding a grudge? Okay, maybe Mom deserved it. But Han didn't. Until this week, she and Mom never discussed Chris. Not even at Christmas and birthdays. It was weird, hearing Mom refer to him again, though she could never bring herself to use Chris's actual name.

"I just saw another item on the news. The organizers are still refusing to cancel the water war competition. A little childish, if you ask me, wasting all that water when there's a drought."

"Everyone needs to be a little childish sometimes," Han said, and left the room before Mom could come up with some smart retort.

Upstairs, she checked the game's Web site. She'd been waiting for an announcement about the end of the game. The details were there. Nothing about her being eliminated. It just said that there were rumored to be three finalists. Presumably her, Chris, and Zorro.

The whole thing would finish tomorrow, in the park.

MAC

Mac checked his mail on Cliff's computer. He found an e-mail addressed to him, Zorro, and Green, sent by the gamekeeper the day before.

> Only three of you remain. One will be left standing to collect the prize at the party on Sunday. To expedite matters, you are ordered to attend the water war at City Park on Saturday. You must stay within the park grounds from midday until you have either won or been assassinated. No spraying before two P.M. I will verify your attendance in person. Have your phone with you and turned on. You may assassinate your opponents in whatever order you choose. Good luck at the conclusion of this historic battle!

This "finale" was also discussed on the game's Web site. It wasn't "sudden death," not exactly. Whether Mac sprayed Green or Zorro first, he could still be taken out by whichever player remained. And the City Park would be full of amateurs with water weapons, so the chances of being sprayed by someone else were high. But the whole thing was fair, he saw that. The game was Mac's to win. He could be the champion on his third attempt. It was an enthralling prospect.

"You don't need us anymore," Shell said, her voice more resigned than bitter.

"You're right, I'm on my own. But if I lose, I'll join you in the water war," Mac said. "It'll be fun to spray people at random instead of always waiting around for a chance to get my target."

"You'd better register then," Cliff said. "Okay, strategy meeting!"

The rules for the water war weren't complex. There were two teams. You were assigned to a team on arrival and given a stapled wristband that changed color, permanently, when it got wet. If the wristband was removed or tampered with in any way, the player was eliminated from the game. The last player to avoid getting soaked was the winner. The game began at two. In previous years, when the main play was over, the water war degenerated into a free-for-all until players got bored or—a distinct possibility this year—they ran out of water.

"Will you really get a wristband?" Shell asked Mac.

"You bet. Taking part in the water war is the best cover I can think of."

Final Saturday 11:30 A.M.
GAMEKEEPER

All of the preparations were in hand. It was another blazing hot day and the city water shortage was irritating, but the three Spray finalists would cope, and the water war players would get by. There was a bigger irritation. The gamekeeper had twice contacted the player called Han. Reluctantly (for the smoke

bomb move turned out to have been rather clever) he had decided to eliminate her. But she didn't appear to have received the
message. Yesterday evening, his first e-mail to her had bounced
back. He reread it now:

> I have received reports that you set off smoke bombs to
> flush your target from his home. This is against the
> spirit and rules of the Spray game. In addition, two of
> your previous targets have complained that you are too
> young to be part of this game and must have faked your
> ID. My assistant says that he had his doubts about your
> age when you were handed your laminate and noted
> this at the time.
>
> I am, therefore, suspending you from the Spray game.
> You have until six P.M. tonight to arrange to see me and
> answer these charges to my satisfaction. Otherwise,
> you will be eliminated from the Spray game.

When she didn't reply to that e-mail, he had sent a second one,
and, as he prepared to leave for City Park, this one, too,
bounced back as "message undeliverable." His last note to her
concluded:

> I am forced, therefore, to expel you from the game. Do
> not be offended by my enforcement of the rules. I hope
> you will still attend the end-of-game party. You'll be sent
> an invitation to the secret venue. This will be mailed to
> your registered address, unless you prefer it to be sent

elsewhere, in which case please inform me of the new
address by Friday morning at the latest.

He looked at the details she had given in when she registered:
real name, Claire Hanoi, age fifteen, address in a dingy part of
the city, high school student. None of it appeared to be true. The
phone number she gave was also dead. If she turned up today,
she could mess up the game. He would have to warn the other
players that she was out but might be around. There were always
one or two mavericks who registered for the game but didn't like
to play by the rules. With luck, even if the girl turned up, she
wouldn't spoil things.

He shut down his computer and set off for the park.

Final Saturday 11:58 A.M.
GREEN

Green walked into the park with Jenny at his side. They had
already visited once, the evening before, and watched the preparations for the day's events. In a sudden-death shoot-out like
this, his girth was a handicap. Planning was everything. He
looked for the gamekeeper.

"Don't worry," Jenny said. She leaned against him, reached
up, and kissed him full on the lips. "You're going to win. I
know it!"

"I've already won if you keep kissing me like that," Green said. Jenny gave him a reassuring smile. Hard to believe, but she really was his girlfriend.

When they reached the middle of the park, near the lake, they stopped and waited. The gamekeeper appeared from behind a tree whose leaves were an unseasonable brown. He held out his hand.

"Congratulations on making it this far. I wanted a chance to speak to each of the players in person before the game begins. I also want to make it clear that there is to be no spraying before two P.M. A hit before then doesn't count. Understood?"

"Understood," Green said.

"And you're on your own. Your friend can watch. She can play in the other water game that's on here today, but she can't help you by hindering or spraying either of your targets."

"Understood," Green said. "How do we verify our kills?"

"Good question. I'll be watching from the city police security cameras."

"They let you use security cameras?" Jenny asked.

"I'm one of the sponsors of the city's annual water game. It's no coincidence that the water war takes place this weekend. But I can't guarantee that I'll see the final, fatal shot. As always, in the Spray game, we operate on mutual trust and respect. If you get sprayed, hand over your laminate and come to the security HQ by the café."

"And if I don't?"

"Then you'll be a worthy winner."

"Have the others arrived? Are they here yet?"

"I saw Zorro a few minutes ago. He's at the edge of the playground, over there. Mac will be here soon. I want to introduce the three of you, go over the rules one last time."

Green and Jenny strolled over to the playground. Zorro sat on a bench, on his own. He had a water pack on his back and wore combat trousers and a khaki T-shirt. On his wrist was a band for the water war game. Green had decided not to get one of those.

"We meet again," Zorro said. "It's been a long three weeks."

"You're a hard man to track down," Green told him.

"That's how I stay alive."

Up close, Zorro was plumper of face than Green remembered, and older: over thirty.

"How many tournaments is this now?" he asked the veteran.

"My sixth. Won three, lost three. And my last, probably."

"Why's that?"

"About to become a dad. Time to put aside childish things."

"Congratulations," Green said, aware that Zorro was looking over his shoulder. "Is the gamekeeper here?"

Zorro nodded. "Hard to tell those two apart from this distance, but I think that's him with Mac."

"People are saying that he's the next you. That he traveled a long way to be in this game."

"Getting to the last three is a good achievement," Zorro told Green. "But it doesn't make Mac me. There's only one me. You, I like. You're an unusual player. Very tactical. You were the assassin I was most scared of."

Green noted Zorro's use of the past tense but said nothing. The gamekeeper and Mac joined them. Hands were shaken. The gamekeeper warned them about a player called Han, who might not realize that she had been expelled from the game. Mac said nothing to Zorro or Green, which was probably wise. It didn't help to get too friendly with your opponents.

"You have the best part of two hours to check the lay of the land, have lunch, do whatever you want," the gamekeeper said. "But you must not leave the park until the game is over. If you do, you lose. Understood? All right. Let the final begin!"

Final Saturday 12:15 P.M.
MAC

Mac left the other contestants and joined Shell, Cliff, and Maiko. All four of them lined up to register for the water war game.

"I can't believe you've come this far," Cliff told him.

"Me neither," Mac said.

"Shell says you've played the game twice before," Maiko said.

"That's right. Never made it to the final week, though."

"Let's hope it's third time's the charm," Shell said, and gave him a quick hug. After they'd got along so well last night, he'd kind of expected more, but Mac didn't really understand girls.

They got their wristbands and separated. Shell and Maiko were assigned red, Cliff and Mac blue.

"You've all got my cell number?" Mac asked. "In case you spot either of my opponents."

All nodded enthusiastically.

"We'll help you if we can," Cliff told Mac, "but remember, all three of us are in this game to win!"

"Me, too," Mac said. "Good luck."

They set off in search of safe cover.

Final Saturday 12:54 P.M.
GREEN

Green's best chance of winning was to hide, and surprise his enemy. The easiest place to hide, Green reckoned, was in plain sight. This was harder for a guy his size but not impossible. He had a plan.

The park had a café, adjacent to the lake in the center, with a gift shop and a small food court. Just behind it was the building in which the game's security HQ was based. The café was where Green waited for the game to begin. Jenny was a foot away, on lookout, waiting near the water war registration table, hidden behind the living statues.

Green had eaten a light lunch, as had Zorro, two tables away. The assassin slipped out when Green wasn't looking. Jenny said she'd seen him heading for the trees, where the blue players were waiting, two or three hundred of them. Neither Green nor Zorro had seen Mac since the gamekeeper introduced them. He certainly wasn't around here.

Green texted Jenny. *It's time.* Then he hurried to the restrooms at the back of the café and waited for her to arrive.

Final Saturday 1:13 P.M.

HAN

Han lined up to get her wristband in the middle of the park. She was nervous. Not because of the age thing—there was no age limit to play in the water war game—but because of the weapon she was carrying. You weren't allowed to carry anything that looked like a real gun.

She didn't talk to anyone else in the line. Most of them were in groups anyhow. She tried not to make eye contact with the three men who stood on pedestals, their bodies painted white. The tall one wore swimming trunks and a turban. The fat one was in a toga, with a laurel wreath around his painted head. The small one was nearest to her height, and wore full Roman armor. For a moment, his heavily made-up eyes caught hers. She looked away. She'd seen these painted people in several places, on vacation and in the city. She always found them creepy. They might not be in the game, she figured, but they were bound to get sprayed at some point. All that white paint and makeup would end up as one hell of a mess.

It took half an hour to get to the front of the line, but once she was there, the stewards didn't inspect her water gun or backpack, they merely took her entry fee (a small donation to charity) and stapled a cloth band to her right wrist. The teams were blue and red. She was on blue. There was three quarters of an hour to go before the game began: plenty of time to find her brother.

The park was a vast area of dried up, dusty ground. The blue players—there seemed to be two or three hundred of them—were congregating on the left-hand side of the park, beyond the dry lake, near the wooded area and the birdcages.

A guy her age began to talk to her. "We've chosen the wrong side. There aren't enough water fountains for refills around here."

"Doesn't matter," Han told him. "Water here's been turned off for weeks."

"That's right," said one of the self-elected leaders. "So conserve every drop you've got for spraying the enemy. If you can't spray, you can't play!"

Han wandered among the players, trying to spot her brother. He was bound to hide himself among these amateurs, these day-trippers of the water wars. Where was Chris?

On a small, makeshift stage, the city's mayor produced a large, stainless-steel whistle from the right breast pocket of his cotton shirt, stepped into the sunshine, and blew it.

The water war was under way.

SHELL

Shell and Maiko fought side by side, charging across the park toward the blue team. As soon as they were all within range of each other, water flowed freely in both directions. Both Shell and Maiko got splashed but not sprayed directly. It was chaotic. Soon, half the players they passed were out of the game. It didn't matter what color your wristband was. Red or blue, once it had been sprayed, the band turned purple. But players kept spraying until they were out of water, then went off in search of more.

Shell used her Super Soaker with care. She wanted to last longer in this game than she had done in the Spray game. Maiko, more exuberant, was soon both eliminated and out of water. She didn't care. The two of them rested by a tree.

"Have you seen Cliff?" Shell asked Maiko.

"No. Think he's with Mac?"

"Dunno. But look over there."

Walking toward them, Super Soaker in hand, was Zorro. The long-haired man wore a red wristband, like them. He and Mac were on opposite sides.

"I'm going to call Mac," Shell told Maiko. "You distract Zorro."

"How?" Maiko asked.

"Remind him that you were his first kill. Offer to team up with him or something. Go now!"

Shell got out her phone and punched in Mac's number on speed dial. She watched Maiko join Zorro. Then a posse of blue players charged over the hill and sprayed the couple from head to toe.

Final Saturday 2:13 P.M.

HAN

The whole thing was a farce. Red players sprayed blue players and vice versa, but team members also sprayed each other for the fun of it. Han made sure that she got sprayed early on. She didn't want to be a target; she wanted to be an onlooker. People kept spraying, even when their wristbands had turned purple. The only thing that stopped people spraying was running out of water. Several had those reserve packs on their backs, feeding water directly into their Super Soakers. They could go on for hours.

At last, Han spotted someone she knew. The guy she saw was driving Mac's car the day that Han sprayed D.C. He was on her brother's team. His wristband was still blue, so he was still in the water war. It was unlikely that he would lead Han to Chris, but she decided to follow him anyway.

GREEN

Green was hot and uncomfortable, but he had a good vantage point, and to move from his position would risk exposure. Everybody in the park looked as hot as him. The day was muggy, with low clouds. All around the café and shops area, families were watching the players as they endlessly sprayed each other. Once the action slowed down, the crowd applauded every time somebody got soaked, probably wishing that somebody would aim a water pistol at them as well.

There were other distractions. Clowns walked by, advertising the circus which began that evening. A bouncy castle had been erected on the dry lake. Someone threw a water balloon in Green's direction and he flinched, but it landed on the smallest of the living statues, the one in Roman armor, who swatted it aside like a fly, then let the water trickle down the gold paint of his breastplate.

Green saw somebody he recognized. It was Zorro, accompanied by the girl whose room Green had visited before the game began, Maiko. Zorro's side was wet, as if he'd just been sprayed. His wristband was purple. What were those two doing together?

Was this Green's best chance of spraying the champion? That depended on the location of Mac. To spray Zorro would be to give himself away. Green decided that he would only spray him if he was spotted. So far, his hiding place was holding up. Green should be safe as long as he stayed still. But that was hard enough to do in this heat, with the sweat gathering and trickling down his back. Not long now, he told himself. Soon, one way or another, it would be over.

Final Saturday 2:21 P.M.
MAC

The couple were in a crowd but Zorro was easy to pick out. He was walking next to Maiko, who was taller than him. Both had been sprayed, which was sensible on Zorro's part. Players with a purple wristband blended in with the crowd. Mac was too proud a player to get sprayed. He and Cliff had cut a swath through the red team, and their wristbands were still bright blue. Shell, on the other side, still had her red wristband. Mac hoped he didn't have to spray her. She was following Maiko and Zorro, keeping Mac informed of their every move. At the moment, they were in a crowd heading toward the café. All were hoping to refill their pistols with water—from the tap if it was working, or failing that, from a water bottle, if there were any left to buy. Most likely Zorro's backpack remained well stocked, but it was impossible to tell.

"This is it!" Cliff told Mac. "You duck behind that tree. I'll steer them your way!"

Mac did as they'd agreed. It was a pincer movement. Cliff

jumped in front of Zorro and Maiko. The crowd moved around them, separating the assassin from the bystanders.

Zorro spoke. "We're already out of the game, man. No point in spraying us."

"Pity," Cliff said. "But that was never my plan. Look behind you."

Zorro tried to run. Neither Cliff nor Maiko stopped him. You weren't allowed assists in the final shoot-out. Anyway, the champion was trapped. Mac's double helix Super Soaker was fully primed and fired a wide spray. The range wasn't as good as some CPS systems, but it was good enough to get Zorro. Soon, the champion was soaked through. He laughed as Mac sprayed him, a good sport to the end.

When Mac was done, the champion bowed to Mac and handed over his laminate.

"You're one hell of a player, my friend. But you still have to beat Green. Good luck with that."

Final Saturday 2:26 P.M.
SHELL

Shell charged through the gaping tourists and retired players, trying to spot any wristbands that were still intact. She was supposed to be looking for Green, too, but he had been invisible since the game began, nearly half an hour ago. She did notice the girl who had sprayed D.C. Han. She must have been eliminated, though, because Mac said there were only three players left. Of course Han was here. Everybody who was interested in water wars was here today.

There was Zorro, walking away from Mac and Cliff, a third-place loser. An ugly thought crossed Shell's mind. An ugly but necessary thought. Why couldn't she be a winner, too? Why was it that in wars, men did all the fighting and women helped on the sidelines: cooks, camp followers, drivers, decoys? What was in this for her? A boyfriend? Now that she thought about it, Shell didn't want a guy like Mac or Cliff to pick her. Why was it men who got to do the asking? She wanted to be a winner. She wanted to be the one who chose.

Mac's and Cliff's wristbands were still blue. Shell was close enough now to spray either of them. She would go for both. Okay, she might only get one before she was eliminated herself. Which to choose? While she was making up her mind, it was made up for her.

"Before we go any further," Cliff said, and Mac turned to him, "I have to do this."

Cliff pointed his pistol. Mac stood there and took it. Cliff shot at the wrist only. Mac's blue wristband turned purple.

"Think you're the last player left?" Mac asked Cliff.

Cliff shrugged, giving the goofy grin that Shell once thought was endearing. Shell stepped forward and, as she did so, Maiko gasped out a warning. Maiko was only a couple of paces away from Cliff. She tried to throw herself in front of him. But Shell was too quick. She sprayed Cliff from top to bottom, soaking his wristband in the process. Cliff shook himself down like a damp dog before speaking to her.

"Shell, Shell. First you wouldn't go out with me, then you spray me as well. Talk about adding insult to injury."

"Nothing personal," Shell replied, but Cliff wasn't looking at her; he was looking behind her.

"Look out!" he shouted.

She looked around. Behind Shell was Han, the girl who got D.C. Wasn't she out of the game?

Up close, Han appeared young: thirteen or fourteen. The gun in her hand looked like a real revolver. Shell pointed her Super Soaker back at her. She still had a little water left in it. But then she noticed that Han's wristband was already purple. And she wasn't pointing the gun at Shell. She was pointing it at Mac.

 Final Saturday 2:29 P.M.
HAN

Han aimed the pistol at the head of the guy who called himself Mac, then paused. For a moment, she thought it was some kind of optical illusion. Chris appeared younger, better looking. Han didn't know what to do. She so badly wanted to press the trigger.

"There's no point in soaking him," the guy from the car

yelled. "Mac told me, you've been . . ." His voice lowered. "Is that a real gun?"

"What is this?" Mac said. "I've been waiting to meet you, Han. Feel free to spray me, but it won't count."

She let the gun drop.

"You're not him," Han said.

"I'm not who?" Mac replied.

"You look like him, from a distance. At least, you look like I thought he'd look after all this time. But you're too young, and your accent is all wrong. You're not Chris. You're not my brother."

"That's right," said a familiar voice from behind her. "He's not Chris. I am."

Han swirled around. Instinctively, she fired. She soaked her brother's T-shirt, then stopped. Chris didn't have a water gun of any kind. He wasn't in the game. Unless . . .

Chris stepped forward.

"My old water pistol," he said. "You kept it."

"Of course I kept it," she said. "I wanted to spray you with it. I was sure you'd be in the game. There can only be one reason why you weren't playing. You're the gamekeeper, aren't you?"

"For the last two years," Chris said. "Sorry it's been so long, sis. I was going to call you when this game was over, I swear."

Han tried not to cry. Her brother stepped forward and tried to embrace her. Han pushed him away. She wasn't into hugs.

Suddenly, lots of people were approaching. The clearing was mobbed. Han expected the crowd to pay attention to Mac, or her brother. But they were all looking at the girl, Shell.

"She's the one!" someone shouted.

"Hold up your arm!" one of the stewards ordered, and Shell did.

"Her band's still red! She's the one!" the steward announced. "We have a winner!"

 Final Saturday 2:41 P.M.
MAC

The center of the park was so crowded that Green could be any-where. The day had turned muggy and overcast. In the gloom, it was hard to spot faces in the crowd. But Green was a big guy. Mac would find him first, as long as he avoided places the assas-sin could hide behind.

Mac had Cliff to one side of him and Maiko on the other. Shell had been escorted away to be feted as the winner of the water war. Mac was proud of her, of course he was, but what she had won paled in significance to what he was on the verge of achieving. Any minute now, he could be champion of Spray on his third attempt. He had already taken out Zorro. Once he got Green, Mac would feel like the king of the world. Mac loved this game. He could play it for the rest of his life. There was a loud rumbling noise nearby.

"I hate to tell you this," Cliff said, "but I think it's going to . . ."

The first drops of rain began to fall, removing the need for

Cliff to finish the sentence. Thunder cracked loudly, just on the other side of the lake. From all over the park, people began to run toward the shop and café, looking for cover.

"First rain in weeks and weeks," Maiko said. "Couldn't it have waited a few more minutes?"

The rain poured, smashing onto the dry, cracked ground.

"Think we should find some cover?" Cliff asked Mac.

"I don't mind being wet," Mac told him. "It's kind of refreshing, don't you think? Mind you, I wouldn't want to be them!"

He pointed at the three living statues, who were still standing on their plinths, watching the crowd run for shelter. The white paint was pouring from their bodies, revealing pale skin beneath. The small one in armor got off his plinth first, holding his shield over his head to act as an umbrella. Then the tall one stepped down from his pedestal. Only then did Mac take a good look at the fat one in the middle. He wore a toga and had a laurel wreath around his head. He looked kind of familiar. The statue reached into his toga and pulled out a tiny red water pistol.

"Sorry, dude," Green said as he pointed the pistol. Before Mac had time to react, the white statue fired the water pistol and landed a direct shot on Mac's head. The game was over.

Third Sunday 8:16 P.M.
MAC

The party was warming up. Chris took Mac to one side.

"I should have won," Mac said. "I was so close, I could taste it."

"It's not about the winning," the gamekeeper told Mac. "It's about how you play. You've got lots of money. You could have done the game the easy way, like Badmonkey, and used hired help. But no, you took the hard way, persuaded people to help you make it to the last two. Respect."

"I plan to enter again, win next time," Mac told him.

"That might be harder than you think," Chris told him. "Zorro's retiring and Green says he's not interested in defending his championship, so you'd be the player to beat. It's a lot harder to win when you're not just another anonymous player."

Behind them, most of the game's two hundred entrants had arrived at the student center. Only one notable player was missing.

"So Han's your sister," Mac said to Chris. "What happened there?"

"Nasty divorce," Chris said. "Six years ago, my mom left my dad for another guy. As soon as I turned sixteen, a couple of months later, I chose to live with my dad. My sister stayed with Mom and her new husband, who was a creep. Dad was a workaholic, built up an even bigger business after Mom left him. He

226

worked himself to death three years ago. And he left me everything. I'm rich. Whereas Mom's second husband spent all of the money she'd got off Dad, then dumped her. I shouldn't have lost touch with them, but I was hurt, and angry. But that's enough about me. What about you? What will you do next?"

Mac shrugged. "No idea. Any suggestions?"

"I do have one, actually. I've been the gamekeeper for two years now, ever since I won the game in Seattle, when I was a student there. Playing the game and then running the game got me through some rough times after Dad died. But I'm through. I've decided to go back to school here and get to know my family again. That means I need somebody to take over from me, someone who loves the game, and can afford to devote a lot of time to it. Somebody like you. Interested?"

"I'm tempted," Mac said.

"No hurry," Chris said. "Whatever you decide, it'll be our secret. Tell me after I've made the presentation. But I really hope you'll do it. I can't think of anyone better, and I hate not to get my way."

Mac looked around the party. He recognized a lot of the guests. There was the Invisible Man, dancing with D.C. A TV game show host was talking to Jal, the schoolteacher. The bald guy who'd been his first assassin was chatting up a fancy, professional-looking woman. Jenny was tucked under Green's left arm. Cliff was kissing Maiko. Shell was in the middle of the dance floor, wearing her water war winner's medal, dancing. . . .

Behind Shell was Zed, whose boyfriend, the policeman, was talking to an old guy in a wheelchair. Zorro was surrounded by well wishers, but sensing Mac's stare, he looked up, twirled his mustache, and gave Mac a friendly smile. At the entrance, Mac saw a young girl arrive. With her hair down and her face mask long gone, Han looked terrific. How old was she? Only two years younger than him. She walked tentatively into the room, looking for someone. Mac gave her a small wave, then turned to her brother.

"I don't need time to decide," Mac told Chris. "I made up my mind. I'll do it. I'll take your place."

"Cool," the gamekeeper replied. "I've got to go now. It's time."

He pushed his way across the dance floor. Han joined Mac.

"Better luck next time," she said.

He grinned at her, suddenly aware of the weight of his new secret. "Will you play again?" he asked her.

"I'm fifteen in November. After that, try and stop me!"

They watched Chris climb onto the stage. The music faded and there were rowdy, tumultuous cheers. Chris switched on the microphone and tapped it once, then called for quiet.

"Ladies and gentlemen, welcome to the grand finale of the Spray game. I'm delighted to say that this year we have a clear, outright winner. Please welcome him to the stage."

The dancers stepped back to create a wide pathway for Green. A mighty roar filled the big room. Two hundred water pistols were raised to the ceiling. The new champion kissed his girlfriend, punched the air, then strode across the floor to claim his prize.

Thank you for reading this FEIWEL AND FRIENDS book.

The Friends who made

SPRAY

possible are:

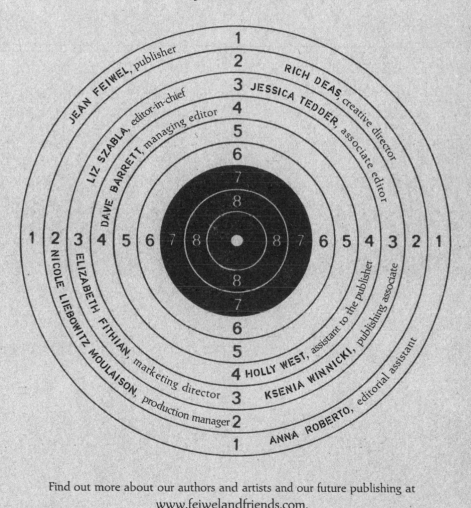

JEAN FEIWEL, publisher

LIZ SZABLA, editor-in-chief

RICH DEAS, creative director

JESSICA TEDDER, associate editor

DAVE BARRETT, managing editor

NICOLE LIEBOWITZ MOULAISON, production manager

ELIZABETH FITHIAN, marketing director

HOLLY WEST, assistant to the publisher

KSENIA WINNICKI, publishing associate

ANNA ROBERTO, editorial assistant

Find out more about our authors and artists and our future publishing at
www.feiwelandfriends.com.

OUR BOOKS ARE FRIENDS FOR LIFE